CHAOTIC ENDEAVORS

AN URBAN ROMANCE STORY

AUBRY J.

Chaotic Endeavors

Published by Grand Penz Publications

SUBSCRIBE

Text Grand to 31996 to stay up to date with new releases, sneak peeks, contest, reading groups and more....

COME JOIN OUR TEAM!!!!

To submit your manuscript to Grand Penz Publications, please send the first three chapters and synopsis to grandpenzpublications@gmail.com

ONE
QUEEN

"There is absolutely nothing wrong with wanting more. Out of everyone, I thought you would be the most excited about me wanting to change my life around." I said, looking at the phone as if she could see me.

"Queen, you are unrealistic. You can't just announce out the blue you are; what did you call it? Changing your life for the best? You are focusing on the wrong thing, find a man young lady. Settle down and start a life that way, besides when is the last time you've been out on a date? Have you been looking into those men I've sent you information on? They are really good picks." My mama said, her unimpressed and almost monotone reply made me want to jump out of a window, but I know not to get upset or better yet allow her to realize she's gotten under my skin.

"I have a list mama, the guy I end up with has the be an amazing man to get me to settle down finally. And to not beat around the bush, I'm not looking to settle down. I want to enjoy my life for the time being." I replied. I could tell that got I'd gotten her attention; she's a control freak; anything new had to be approved by her. No matter that

I'm grown and haven't lived at home in years, she still felt the need to try and control my entire life. I'm supposed to be the strategic one, yet she played the life like a grand-master chess player.

"What do you mean you have a list that you go by when you're dealing with a potential man?" My mama said like always; she completely ignored the second part of my statement. As I worked through cleaning out my closet, I tried to prepare myself for what she was about to say mentally. I'd only be in town for about a week, and after that, I was on the road again. If I didn't do it now, I'd find an excuse to do it later, and with my luck, it would be six months from now.

"Exactly what I said, mama, I have a list more like standards that I have set for whoever I end up with. Is that not okay? I mean, I highly doubt you saw daddy and was like oh he's cute. I'll marry him and pop out some kids along the way." Pulling down shirts, I know I'm never going to wear again, I threw them towards the pile I had sitting near the door. More than half my closet sat in one of those piles that would be donated to a local charity.

"No smart ass I didn't, but I also didn't have a ridiculous list of demands to compare them too." I stopped what I was doing and looked over my shoulder to the phone as if she could see me. Shaking my head, I went back to fold my stack of orange t-shirts. If she could have seen me, she would know I felt like her statement was a little on the judgmental side but then again knowing her she wouldn't care.

"How can you say they are a ridiculous list of demands when you haven't even asked what they are. I have requirements. You can't blame me for wanting nothing but the best for myself." There was no reason to try and further my explanation; it was logical to want the best in a partner. Which, in turn, would bring the best out of you, who wouldn't want the best brought out of them by the person they chose to live their life with?

"Okay, give me the list if it's not ridiculous."

"Fine." Standing up, I brushed my clothes free of any lint and leaned against the island that sat in the middle of the closet. It housed my shoes in the bottom and on top lay different pieces of jewelry that I never wore. I crossed my arms over my chest and began listing off my requirements. "He has to be tall, smart both street and book smart. Funny, honest, excellent hygiene, and that includes dental because you know a great smile can go a long way. Dark, like Hersey chocolate, I'm okay with a dad's bod; I have a body and sorry, not sorry, but I don't want a twig poking me in my back and side when he's trying to cuddle. Goal orientated because I can't carry him. Protective, logical in his decisions, but I need emotion as well, or should I say passion? He needs to understand emotions in a man is not a weak trait to have and display."

"He sounds like a dream and a fantasy." She interrupted me to say.

"He has to love me, mama, like me. That love that I can feel when I'm near him. He must make my soul ache for him. I'm not dumb I understand that things like that take time, but I must be able to look at him and know that any fear that I have he can conquered them. "I'm not selfish, so I would want him to understand that everything he does for me, I'll do the same for him." I said with so much passion; I scared myself for a second. I chose not to react to her comment because I wasn't in the mood to argue.

"Girl, you want what you young people call a book bae, an unrealistic man who comes out of nowhere and sweeps you off your feet. You haven't allowed yourself the luxury of fantasy in your entire life. It's always been logic and strategy. I highly doubt you even know how to receive a man like that if he fell right into your lap." Her attitude was evident over the phone; I could picture her rolling her eyes and shaking her head as she spoke. As she spoke, I could picture her opening the curtains in the living room, allowing all the natural sunlight to come into the house. House spotless as if it were going to be a picture in a magazine.

"Yeah thanks for the pep talk, you're a great support system, mama." I dropped my head; she knew exactly how to kill any joy I had. She was right, even though I wouldn't admit it to her.

"I'm not trying to take away from what you think you want Queen, but you have, to be honest with yourself. You're damn near thirty, no kids, finishing up one silly job to finally get into a career. You have to set your standards to a realistic expectation, or you'll be single for the rest of your life."

I looked at my phone again, this time I wouldn't even respond to the dismissive attitude she had towards me. It would never be good enough; I was the child who never measured up. Which was okay because I never competed with my siblings, their success or lack thereof was on them.

"Mama I gotta go, I promised Parker I would meet up with her later on today for some girl time before its time to hit the road again." I headed towards the other side of the island towards the phone as I talked to her.

"Queen honey look, all I'm saying is you have to look at your future, you're almost thirty, beautiful and could be considered a catch if you got your head out those books enough to realize it. It's just you lack the social skills to meet someone which I can understand since you wasted most of your time playing that stupid game."

"I lack social skills? Ma what are you talking about?" I

stopped mid-stride, trying to understand where this was coming from. I socialized with people all the time. Even when I did not want to.

"I spoke with your sister, and she said during her wedding you outright refused to dance with Jason's groomsmen, you know the one who you walked down the aisle with. Well anyway, she said no matter how many times he asked you told him no." She huffed into the phone as if it was her, that I had refused.

"That's because he kept trying to grope me every time we were within reaching distance! Did Tempest also tell you that Jason's uncle, who was there, had to take him home because he got so drunk, he was trying to strip in the foyer?"

"Are you going through a phase like Tommy?" She said as she completely ignored my response once again. Knowing her, she had made her way to the kitchen, breakfast, and lunch long gone and forgotten; dishes washed now it was time to prepare dinner. My parents had a set time for everything, yet she had the nerve to talk about me and my list.

"Ma. What phase is Tommy going through?" Dropping my head down on the island, I couldn't wait to hear her response so I could tell Tommy.

"You know, Tommy likes girls Queen." She whispered as if she was telling some type of long-buried family secret.

"Ma' she does not and has never liked girls. Who told you that?" I wanted to laugh, I did, but it was almost pathetic to hear my mother decide my sister like girls when we all knew she didn't. And even if she did, what would be wrong with that?

"Well, how else do you explain her obsession with basketball? She's never around any men, nor has she brought anyone home. She lives and breathes that stupid game. It's been that way for as long as I can remember." She sounded offended at the thought of Tommy enjoying a sport; I remember as a kid that's all Tommy did was play with my brother and cousins. She was good, and she enjoyed it, but our mother didn't care about that part. All she cared about was Tommy hated dressing up and would rather be in shorts and a t-shirt all day. Tommy's style didn't fit into the society look she tried to give off. But Tommy didn't care, like at all, there were times when she would purposely dress and act a certain way to get on my mother's nerves.

"Ma Tommy doesn't like girls, trust me. Okay?" I didn't want to argue more with her about my sister's sex life. It was wasted breath.

"Oh, honey, if you say so." She had dismissed entirely everything I'd said, if we were face to face I'm pretty sure she would have patted me on the head and spoke to me slowly like I had a problem understanding what she was trying to tell me. "But back to you, It's time to settle down, get you a respectable man, maybe Parker could introduce you to one of her doctor friends. Didn't you say last time there was someone interested in you? Whatever happened to him, you know the dentist?"

"We are fuck buddies, and that's all. He's boring, very condescending and slightly controlling, and if you want me to be honest, his sex isn't all that great. I mean, I get my nut off, but that's it." I answered her honestly. Over the years, I learned not to beat around the bush with her. Even though I was the least likely of her children to argue with her. I took the high road and usually ignored her snarky comments and obsessive behavior regarding my personal life. But sometimes I got the upper hand and said something to ruffle her feathers, which always gave me a point on the invisible scoreboard that only I kept score on.

"You could've said you weren't interested in him, that would've sufficed, you didn't have to be so crude. I'll see you later on next week, be on time, and do not intentionally miss your flight like you did last time," She said and hung up the phone. Shrugging I raised off the island, grabbed my phone, and went back into the master bedroom. I'd done all the cleaning I planned to do that day. Laughing I thought about what she said; I hadn't intentionally missed my flight last time I had made it into town early, after checking into my hotel room I decided to ignore her calls and sleep for a little. When I met up with her and the rest of my family later that day, she assumed I'd missed my flight, and I didn't see the point of correcting her. I scrolled through my contact list and sent my sister a text as I sat down on my bed. Whenever one of us had the pleasure of speaking with our mother, we would text whoever became a topic of our conversations.

Me: Yo, mama, think you gay!

Tommy: Man! That woman is slower than molasses. How did she come to that conclusion?

Me: Your love for basketball.

Tommy: I love technology too, but she doesn't say anything about that though lol. See you next week!

Me: Bye!

Tommy: And don't be late either!

Me: I'll see what I can do!

I HEARD the ding of the timer telling me it was time to change partners from the other side of the room. I'd let my friends talk me into doing this and let me tell you now; this was by far the dumbest thing I'd ever done in my twenty-nine years of living. I had other things I could be doing because one thing for certain and two things for sure sitting in this chair listening to some man lie and try to impress me with material things wasn't it by a long shot. It wasn't how I pictured my life going; it wasn't what I wanted to do with my time honestly. I'd rather be sitting on my couch doing a crossword puzzle with the television on as background noise. This wasn't it, not by a long shot.

Glancing over I could hear Parker laughing at something number seven had said to her, that's how I remembered them, by numbers. He was number seven, from what I could tell he was more than likely was married, his tan line on his ring finger was a dead giveaway, and when I mentioned it, he quickly pulled his hand away from the table and tried to change the subject. After that I tuned him out, I didn't do married men, it was a rule. Before him were six other men, each more annoying than the last. All of them wasted my time, number one's teeth were so yellow I was sure he ate a stick of butter before he showed up. Number two's phone kept ringing; after the ninth time, I excused myself to go to the bathroom. I never came back to the table. Number three stuttered, now don't get me wrong, I usually would be okay with someone who had a stutter, but for some reason, his voice started to make my eye twitch. Number four's clothes were entirely to tight; I could see his pulse through the collar of his shirt. Number five kept licking his hand, trying to smooth his hair over his bald spot. Good ole number six now he took the cake, he had to be maybe 60 and told me right off the bat he was looking for someone who could handle him on his little blue pill. I didn't know if I was supposed to cry or laugh, so I yelled for time to be over and jetted out of the meeting room faster than I could imagine. I know I probably looked crazy as hell to everyone in there, but I didn't care. This shit was for the birds and I wasn't a bird.

When Parker made eye contact with me, I mouthed, "This shit is dumb," which prompted her to laugh louder and walk to the other side of the room. She'd seen my struggle list of dates and couldn't be trusted not to allow this shit to keep happening, a small part of me wonders if she set this up on purpose as some time of revenge ploy. I'd give her another thirty minutes before I left her, the whole girl code of leaving with the same number of people you came with was out the window.This wasn't my scene, and I'd only done this to shut her and a few other of our friends up.

"Well you gotta be the hottest thang walking, how are you doing?" Without looking up, I knew whoever this man was that decided to his ass down at the table I had occupied in the back of the room wasn't going to last longer than a few seconds. For one he had a smell, I wasn't sure if it was coming from his mouth or another part of his body, but I know one thing for sure and two things for certain I refused to deal with it. "Shit look at your eyes, girl, don't you know with as dark as you are you pulling off those colored contacts!" He'd damn near yelled at the top of his lungs; of course, I would explain to him that they weren't contacts but what was the point? He'd never believe me, and I'm sure if I pronounced the medical term for what I had, he wouldn't understand what I said, so I'd rather say nothing. Like at all, if I sat here long enough, he would have to understand I wasn't interested.Right?

"Wrong, you were dead ass wrong for taking me to that thing. I don't care what your excuse is Parker; it was wrong."

"You didn't have to just stare at the man Queen, I mean hell he thought you were having a stroke or something. He looked so scared." We were back at my house after the last guy with the odor sat down at my table. I was done. I mentally clocked out and sat there until he started hollering for help. She wasn't lying. He did think I stroked out, and maybe a small part of me did because the entire time he sat there smelling like year-old ass, I didn't say a word. Not when he asked me my name, or anything else. I just sat there; I reminded myself to blink every few seconds and just let him talk. When Parker made her way back over to my table, she took one look at me and laughed louder than he was yelling for help. She knew what I was doing; she'd seen me do it plenty of times over our friendship. I'd developed this habit over the years of just mentally shutting down. My face would go blank, and my eyes would slowly blink every few seconds. Mentally I was aware of everything going on around me, but I just refused to acknowledge anything around me with a response, verbally or otherwise.

"He smelled." It was a simple response, but she understood completely what I was getting at. It was another one of those things that were on my list. You couldn't have an odor; hygiene is extremely important to me.

"He didn't smell." Flopping down on the other end of my couch, I watched as she typed away at her phone, more than likely talking to someone she'd met at that horror show that they called speed dating.

"Yes, he did, I smelled him before I even saw his face." Leaning backward on the arm of the couch, I reached for the remote as we talked. I needed noise in the background. I hated silence; I dealt with it enough; I didn't want to deal with it if I didn't have to. Even though Parker was loud enough to drown out the silence, I still didn't want to take the risk.

"What did he smell like?" Rolling her eyes, she sat her

phone down, whomever it was had been officially dismissed and more than likely would never hear from her again.

"Ass." Flipping through the channels, I settled on one of those shows about buying houses; I could never understand a young couple could have stupid jobs like dog walker and twine roller and a budget of seven hundred thousand dollars. I mean, don't get me wrong; I could because generational wealth was a hell of a thing, but they still had stupid jobs.

"That man did not smell like ass, maybe musty balls but definitely not ass. I smelled him when I walked over to you after I heard him yelling like a damn banshee." Smirking, she relaxed further into the couch and slid out of her shoes. "He definitely had some lungs on him."

"If you knew then why you ask?"

"To see what you describe it as." Flipping her head over into her lap, she started pulling her massive amount of hair into a high ponytail. The lion's mane as she likes to call it sat bigger than her head with curls of natural red hair framing her face. "Anyway, what's on the itinerary for your leave/family gathering before your last tournament?"

"I pack tomorrow and leave Friday. I'll be in New York to meet up with my parental unit for a day or two since they want to meet up at the border for a little family time. Then fly out to the grands on Sunday. Spend two days with them, then Tuesday night I'll fly out for the tournament, sleep for 16 hours straight, and play on Thursday morning. Hopefully, this won't be an all-day thing, a half-day max." Rolling my shoulders, I tried to ease the stress of spending so much time with my family. The conversation with my mom from earlier today still played over and over in my head. One of my siblings was married, but she looked at me for the one to give her a grandchild first. Every time we saw each other, it was the same constant reminder that my biological clock was ticking, and I was wasting potential grandchildren with every menstrual cycle I had.

"How are you going to handle your mom and her nagging?"

"Ignore her until she's blue in the face or my father rescue me from the death grip of relentless questioning his wife subjects me to."

"Yeah, right, that'll never happen." Laughing, she made her way to the kitchen and grabbed a water bottle out of the fridge. "You may as well give in and have a kid; hell adopt a puppy, and I'm fairly sure she'll shut up for a little while; she may think you're lonely."

"A kid doesn't change loneliness."

"True, but it will give peace of mind, especially since you're retiring soon and will have a lot more free time on your hands. She sees you letting go of the one dream you've had since childhood. You dominated a sport that black people aren't even considered worthy opponents for most of the time. And you did it at a young age. Girl please your mama is worried you're going to get bored, call her up and tell her you changed your mind and you're going back to playing." Shrugging, she got back comfortable on the couch; of course, she would analyze the situation and see exactly how my mother's fears were rational even if her expectations weren't.

"Thanks, doc, you saved me thousands in therapy bills." Sarcastically I smiled brightly at her, and this time, she rolled her eyes. "But don't worry about me going back we all know once I'm done, I'm done. This is getting marked off my list."

"How could I forget about your list? Between that list and rules, you're set for life, aren't you?" This time it was her sarcasm that was being shot across the room, she may hate my list and rules, but they have kept me sane all these years, so they were staying even if everyone else hated them. "One day, you're going to meet someone who is going to throw that damn list and all your rules straight to hell."

"You wish that on me?"

"You know what I want you to do?" From the look on her face I could tell her mind was already running a thousand different scenarios. Each one more than likely more outlandish than the last.

"What?"

"I want you to be open to the next guy you meet," She said as she flipped through the channels on TV. "I mean like real open, don't pull back and just enjoy him. If you don't know what to do, just think of me and go with whatever you think I would do and run with it. But that means stepping out of your usual box and going with the flow. Don't try to control the situation. This isn't a chess match."

Chance

The constant buzz of my alarm going off finally pulled me out of my sleep, being able to turn off the alarm proved to be a whole different matter to deal with. Some chicks arm was thrown across my upper body, and I'm just going to assume another one's legs were across my lower half, and the only reason I could tell it was two different women was that they were two different shades of brown.

"Ladies, " Shaking them gently, I tried to get them to wake up, but I could tell this was going to be a problem. I heard her before I saw her, the click of the six-inch heels she always seemed to wear was coming closer and closer to my door. "Ladies, come on, you gotta get up because if she catches you in here, it's going to be trouble you don't want."

One pulled her head from under the covers, her make up is smeared and her leave out on her lace front sticking out from any and every direction. "Are you married?" Her high-pitched voice spiked with worry as she looked around the room, I'm guessing for her clothes. She jumped out of bed, but her friend is still sleeping under the covers; her lite snores could be heard. She was cute but not the type I could see myself with, but what I could remember from last night, her head game was something vicious.

"Nah ma, I'm not married, but the woman who's about to bust up in here is going to throw you out, and she does not care if you have on clothes or not." Grabbing what I assumed was her dress, I watched as she threw it on and hurriedly grabbed her friend's dress and threw it to her. She was half awake, trying to figure out what her friend was doing rushing around. Chick number two was more my type on looks; she reminded me of K. Michelle, post-surgery body before it got all fucked up, and she had to get it all taken out. Baby girl's arch was amazing; if Jess weren't on her way in here, I'd bend her ass right over and get a replay of last night.

"Stevie get your ass up and get dress; his wife is on her way in here with his lying ass." Chick one said, which caused her friend to jump up and started getting dressed too. As they were doing their thing, I grabbed my shorts off the side of the bed and pulled them on. The last thing I wanted to do was hear Jess's mouth about my lack of clothing.

Just as they were putting on their shoes, Jess threw open the door, which caused them to squeal a little from the force of the door hitting the wall. She didn't even stop to look at them, just pointed to the door as she walked over to the windows to pull open the blinds. They quickly took off, but Stevie looked back, and I winked at her, which caused her to blush.

"Do you even know their names this time?"

"The one who left last name is Stevie, her friend I have no clue." I said as I walked towards the bathroom, I heard her laugh softly as she exited the room. Jess was my saving grace a lot of times after a long night at the club. She knew the drill, come in around 9, make a small scene, scare them off, and go on about her day. Sometimes they would make a fuss, but she will ignore them and go on about her life. The one's who did not cause a fuss I usually send a quick text later that day telling them how sorry I was for my sister in law barging in and would make it up to them later. Stevie was definitely going to get a text later on today.

After doing my normal morning routine, I headed downstairs to the tattoo shop that I lived above. C&C Tattoo has been in business coming up on ten years, and we had made a name for ourselves. Between my brother and I, we kept the shop busy, but it was Jess's business savvy skills that kept our calendars jam-packed for months on out. She always had our names out there, and we stayed doing somebody's tattoo convention. She even hustled my artwork on the side through social media. It wasn't too much in this industry that we didn't have our hands in because of her. Hell, last year I even did and won one of those reality TV shows about tattoo artists.

"Morning my good people," Hoping off the last step, I made my way over to the scheduling desk to see how many people I had booked today. We opened up in about an hour to do some private tattoos and a few piercing. Walk in's, piercings, and appointment tattoos would start rolling in in about three hours.

"Man, stop using my woman as a shield to keep your groupies away. She has barely been back in town a week." Channing my older by a mere 11 months brother said as I sat down at the desk. We joked around a lot with our parents about the fact that we were considered ghetto twins. Of course, he acted like he was my daddy instead of my brother, but I let him get away with it because he looked out for me growing up. It wasn't too much he did that I couldn't do, and when his boys complained about me riding, he put them in their place and dared them to say something about it. Now that we were grown, we still kicked it with each all the time; we were business partners and brothers, it was a good thing we got along so well.

"I didn't even know Jess was back in town yet, so how was I using her, huh?" Glancing up, I shot him a look just to see his reaction. As much as I love Jess and thought she was a great businesswoman, she tended to jump ship whenever the mood hit her. I'm not sure why he put up with it, but yeah, if he liked it, then I loved it.

"Yeah alright." Waving me off, he went back to his drawing, he was doing to prepare for his next client. "We still have to check out the shop. Did you want me to do it, or will you do it later?"

"That's on yall; I already told you I'm just there to establish rules and show the new kids how we do thing. I'm thinking about bringing in someone from one of the other sites to help out but I'm not sure yet. But just so you know before that I'm taking a much-needed vacation. Work on some of my private pieces that I plan to sell and stack this money." Hopping up from the desk, I made my way into the back where my booth is. They could keep the leg work to themselves; I was more hands-on and would rather keep it that way. It worked out for our other two locations, so to me, it was no reason to change it.

"I don't see why that boy allows her to just up and disappear whenever she wants to." My dad looked up from under the hood of his 65 mustangs he has been restoring for the last six years. He did it in his free time to get away from my mama when she was getting on his nerves. He thought it was a secret, but she knew, and she had no problem getting on his nerves when she needed a little free time to shop with my aunts. "You can't be the man of your home when your woman just up and runs away every time she feels like it. How long was she gone this time? Three weeks? Just up and left him on a Tuesday, said she would be back. Grabbed her damn go-bag, she had sitting in the closet like she was a pregnant woman preparing to go into labor any damn day and ran off."

I listened to him bitch about Channing and Jess relationship like he did every time she popped back up. I tried to explain to him years ago that Channing couldn't control her just like he couldn't control mama, but he told me to shut the hell up and get a woman first, so I left it alone. But it was true Channing couldn't make her stay if she needed to leave, he'd tried once, and I swear the girl had have been a ninja or assassin in another life because she picked the lock and scaled the side of the house to get away before we even knew she was gone. After that, Channing stopped trying, told her that he'd be there when she turned her location back on no matter how far she went. He was a better man than me, I wouldn't try to keep something that refused to be kept no matter how much I love her.

"Pops man let it go, they will be here in a little, and you know how he is, you say the wrong thing, and he shuts down for weeks. I don't have time to pull him out his pity party, we are opening another shop in a few weeks I need his head in the game."

"That nigga need to be going to therapy not opening up a new shop." Throwing his wrench, he slid from under the car. Huffing the entire damn time, dude couldn't let it go if his life depended on it. Out the corner of my eye I watched as Channing pulled up on his bike with Jess behind him.

"Behave man."

"Shut up, this my damn house." After helping him up, I watched as he wiped the oil off his hand and made his way over to them. Yeah, this was going to be a long-ass night. I hoped my mama cooked enough for me to take a decent amount home because I could already tell this nigga was not about to let shit be.

TWO
QUEEN

Forty-eight hours, that's all I was giving myself to have to deal with my parents, well, mainly my mother. My father, I could deal with and have absolutely no problems with. But that wife of his, that woman could drive me to drink and then some. For as far back as I could remember we'd had a strained relationship, I couldn't pinpoint a time when we could be in the same room with each other for longer than ten minutes without some type of argument happening. My dad said it was because she wanted the best for me, but she didn't know how to go about saying it. I didn't believe him.

Growing up she was a very supportive parent. But as I got older, she showed her face less and less, and when she called, it was always to nag about something she didn't like. I'd grown accustomed to the negative, yet I didn't accept it, so I stayed away unless my dad asked me to come to see him. She often complained that my dad and grandparents spoiled me, and it was true I am spoiled, but I've worked for everything that I've ever gotten. What she didn't want to admit was that she was spoiled as well, by everyone.

"Queen, have you given any thought about what you

will be doing once you retire?" Mama said from her side of the table. Her posture perfect, make up flawless and not a hair out of place. Her outfit for the day was a hunter green, deep V linen-blend jumpsuit that she paired with some simple black sandals. Compared to my choice of black yoga pants, white fitted top, and tennis shoes, she looked like she about to jump right onto someone's runway.

"Teaching, I told you this the last time we spoke. I start in a few months." Looking over the menu, I waited for her lackluster response. It was always the same; she hated that I was working at an underprivileged school instead of a private school or charter. She was a product of a private school while my father insisted and eventually won the argument of sending us to public school because that is where he went. He told her it gave us a better experience dealing with real life, and he was right. We'd all made it out, attested to the fact that it was one teacher that sealed our fate and pushed us harder to succeed. Even with them being hands-on and active in almost everything we did. It was one teacher for us all that sealed our fate on loving or hating school. For me, it was my second-grade teacher, Mrs. Robinson, she had instructed the class that we all had to pick a program for school to be apart of the entire year. I knew it was coming, had seen my older siblings come home and complain about having to do it. I was set on picking robotics, but when the list got to me, and I realized all the other kids had the same idea, and it was already full, and the only thing left was either chess or band I so heartbroken. I cried. I had no interest in playing any kind of instrument, and Mrs. Robinson knew that so she told me to sign up for Chess but I wasn't interested in that either. She called my parents and informed them of my disinterest in the game and gave them my option of either chess or band.

When I got home, my dad sat me down after dinner and pulled out the chessboard, taught me how to play, and let me know if I could beat him in a game he would pull some strings in getting me on the robotics team. I practiced for weeks, even enlisted my grandparents on practicing with me. Everyday after school I sat in practice pouting that I wasn't getting my way, then I'd go home and play against my family. Before I knew it the season was halfway over, and even though I was good, I still hadn't beat my dad. No matter how much I tried, got frustrated and cried for him to let me win, he never did. By the end of second grade, I had bested most of the kids in the district and was making a name for myself.

I also had fallen in love with the game. When the school year was over, I begged my parents to sign me up for every tournament I could find. And with the help of my grandparents they sent me to everything they could find. If there wasn't a tournament I sat in the park and played against all the older people who met up to play. To this day I thank Mrs. Robinson for calling my parents because I found a game that I loved.

"Do you know what grade?" My daddy asked, taking control of the conversation. I'm pretty sure my mother had informed him of our discussion from late last week. He usually stayed out of our disagreements and tried to steer the conversation into a different direction as much as possible.

"Third grade, I may even sign up to teach chess." Sipping my water, I watched as my mom rolled her eyes. I couldn't say she hated the fact that I played, I think she hated that it took me away from her so much growing up and in adulthood. But it also paid for my college education. Although my parents were not hurting for money, it was still a blessing they did not have to pay for my schooling.

"You can't stay away even if you tried." My father chuckled and went back to his food. He didn't care what I did. My happiness and safety were all that matter to him. It was an difference in their approach to us. My dad let us live our lives the best way we saw fit. While my mom wanted us to act a certain way, say certain things. The way people perceived us was more important than who we were to her. I guess growing up with money made you a little more pretentious than growing up without it.

"Your next step should be finding a husband." She said as the waitress filled our glasses. Glancing over at her, I tried not to roll my eyes.

"I am not worried about a husband." I said, trying to control my temper. I adjusted my ponytail to try and distract myself.

"You need to be. I don't know how many times I've told you that you're not getting any younger." She said as she flicked an invisible piece of lint off the table. Her dark gaze is traveling around the room before they settled on me as she waited for my response.

"I've ever much aware of my age."

"So, act like it! Find a husband Queen; it's time." The tone she used reminded me of a parent trying to explain something to their child, and they were at the end of their rope.

"I told you already it's not on my list of things to do right now." I said, this time, I was looking around the room, mainly looking for the waitress so I could get the check, pay, and leave. Her and this marriage talk would eventually drive me crazy.

"Queen." The way she said my name and the deep sigh

that followed was wrecking my nerves more. I was the child who was never enough. No matter what I did or who I became, I still wouldn't live up to her expectations.

"Ma'am," I said as I finally was able to locate our waitress and wave her over.

"You are starting to piss me off." She informed me.

"The feeling is mutual." I shot back quickly, snapping my eyes back to her. Her taken back expression would've been funny if she was anyone else. Usually, I didn't say anything or allow her to get the best of me, but today I wasn't in the mood for it or her. The fact that she saw nothing wrong with her constant picking at the topic was beyond me at this point.

"Look, mama; I love you. I do, but this conversation is not needed, nor will it continue. If you can't respect my choices, then stop bringing up the conversation. You got Tempest married off with no problem, enjoy that." I said, standing up, I pushed my chair in, grabbed my purse, kissed my father on the cheek, and left before she could say another word. I headed back to my hotel room for a much-needed nap. As soon as my head hit the pillow I was out.

The constant pounding on my door, followed by a deep laugh, woke me up out a deep sleep. Pulling the covers back, I climbed out the bed and made my way to the door. Pulling it open, I smiled at the sight of my brother standing there. Emanuel McDaniel looked exactly like our father, standing at six foot even, with skin as dark as mine, two-tones locs, full beard, full lips, slightly pointed nose, dark eyes, thick eyebrows, and a smile that made women stop and stare.. Pulling me into a hug, we swayed side to side laughing, undoubtedly happy to see each other. Letting me go, he grabbed my face gently and kissed my forehead. For as long as I could remember, he always greeted me the same way..

Growing up, he had been my safety net and best friend. Now we hardly saw each other because of our busy work schedule, but we text daily.

"What are you doing here?" I asked as we walked back into my room.

"I talked to pops last night, and he told me that you guys were meeting here this time, and I had a last-minute cancelation on my schedule, so I hoped on a flight this morning, and here I am." He said, taking a seat on the couch. He stretched his long frame out and crossed his ankles. The all-black Nike joggers and the fitted yellow tank looked good against his skin.

"You mean she didn't tell you about it?" I said, referring to our mother; they'd had a big falling out years ago when she found out exactly what his business was. Over the years, Emanuel told her that he invested in a few start-up businesses and left it at that. It wasn't until about five years ago she found out that one of those start up businesses was actually an exclusive BDSM club. She had disowned him and hadn't spoken to him since, how she found out we will never know.. It was only recently that she started to speak to him even though he and our dad spoke daily.

"You already know she didn't. The last time we spoke, she called to tell me that it was time to let my foolish business go and that I needed to settle down. When I told her no, she hung up on me and blocked my number." He said, shrugging his shoulders.

"I'm sorry," I said sadly as I thought about how Emanuel had been treated over the years.

"Hey, don't worry about it." He said, waving off the melancholy that was bound to set in if we continued with the conversation. "So, are you ready to get this final win under your belt?" He said as he smiled.

"Yep, no joke. I was a little sad this morning about this being the end, but then I remembered I'll get to be at home permanently. That means stability, and you know how long I've wanted that." I said getting comfortable on the other couch.

"True." He said, nodding his head.

"Oh, have you found a house yet? I know you said you started looking not too long ago, but you hadn't mentioned anything in a while." I asked.

"Yep, I close on it in a few weeks; I'll be in town for a few days to take care of that, then Kory and I will be permanent residents of Clarksville." He said smiling even harder. A few months ago, he had mentioned he was ready to find a permanent residence because his daughter Korton who we called Kory, would be starting kindergarten. I had mentioned Clarksville just to give him closure, never did I imagine that he would agree to it. "I even spoke with Anlee about decorating for me, thankfully she agreed. Kory's even excited and you know how she gets when she gets her mind set on something."

"You already know I do; I have to make sure she and Harlem hang out." I said, laughing, the look of pure horror of having Kory with Harlem evident on his face.

"As long as you keep Parker's crazy ass in check I don't care." He said as he adjusted in his seat while pulling his loc's from behind him so he wouldn't be leaning against them.

"You haven't seen her since she's gotten custody of Harlem, she's mellowed out majorly." I said laughing, the skeptical look he gave me caused me to laugh harder.

Emanuel had stayed for a few more hours talking before he made his way back to the airport. His trip short-lived because he had to get back before Kory's maternal grandparents back to him. He had been raising her as a full-time single father after her mom Kasey got a job offer overseas working for an accounting firm. He told her his daughter would not be going, and she signed over all her rights without looking back. From time to time, she would pop up and try to make her presence known, but even at the age of seven, Kory couldn't care less about her. The support system she had between our family and Kory's other grandparents made it to were she wanted for nothing, and the lack of her mother being present played no significant impact on her life.

Later that night, I folded my clothes neatly back into my suitcase as my sisters sat on the other side of the room and bickered back and forth as only sisters could do. After Emanuel left, I decided to change my flight and visit my grandparents earlier than I originally expected. I was in no mood to deal with the shitty attitude I already knew my mom would have. I was due to be at the airport in about three hours, so I spent my time with my sisters catching up.

"Queen, can you please tell your sister that her constant nagging only reminds us of her mother." Tommy, my oldest sister, said as she tossed her basketball into the air as she lay against the arm of the couch. At 33, she was just getting back to the swing of things after living overseas for the last ten years playing basketball in Italy. Even with the growing popularity of the WNBA, she never had the desire to play for them. She often said she got paid more money and had better respect there than she did here.

"I'm not nagging. All I'm asking is when is Queen going to settle down.I don't think it's a question that is intrusive or uncalled for." Tempest, our youngest sister, asked from her spot on the floor. She was doing some type of headstand against the wall. Her eyes closed as she tried to relax. Out of us all, she looked and sadly acted like our mother the most. It was her hippy personality that set them apart. But as of lately, she was starting to change. I don't know if it was because of her husband or being around our mother more. Tommy and I weren't sure.

"You sound like mama with all the questions. Maybe Queen isn't ready to settle down, ever thought about that?"

"Maybe Queen isn't ready to settle down because she hasn't found the right man yet." Popping her eyes open, Tempest looked over at me and then at Tommy. The right man? What year were we in? Who said I was even ready to be with someone or even looking?

"You've been married for seven weeks, and now you're trying to marry her off too? She's literally been playing Chess for the last 20 years. She has one more tournament left, let her play that without you and mama beating down her door with prospective husbands."

"I guess you're right." Flipping over to get into the upright position, Tempest fixed her clothes and smiled at me. "Plus, we all know Queen has a list of Dont's a mile long that a man has to pass before she would even consider dating him."

I STOOD next to the ticket taker laughing as she not so quietly went on and on about a customer who had refused to check his carry-on bag that was obvious over the weight limit. He struggled to carry it but swore it wasn't over the limit. To make matters worse, he attempted to prove her wrong by trying to lift it over his head. He had failed miserably and only complained more about how unfair it was that he was forced to spend the extra fifty-five dollars to check his bag. It was only after she offered to do it for free that he shut up.

"You know he would've continued to complain until he got his way." I said to her as she shook her head and typed away at her scanner.

"I know which is why I comped him so that he would shut up. I am not in the mood at all." She said as she continued to work. Over the last twelve years, I'd used the same airline and had gotten to know a lot of the airport workers from my constant traveling. Miranda had worked this gate for nearly six of those twelve years, and we always chatted as away to pass the time.

"You know I'm going to miss seeing your face, right? Like whom am I going to laugh with when these crazy-ass flights are delayed?" She said, looking up at me. Her eyes are watery with unshed tears that she was trying to hold back.

"You have my number Miranda and all of my social media contacts." I said, smiling my way through the thought of me dropping a few tears too.

"I know, it's just going to be different is all." She said shrugging as she wiped the tears that managed to escape away quickly. We both turned our heads towards the intercom as my flight was called. I held my arms out for a hug which she quickly returned. Letting her go, I turned around to pick my bag up off the floor; I cleaned my glasses with the bottom on my shirt. I looked at Miranda one last time and headed into the walkway.

THREE
CHANCE

"Nigga did you see her ass, though?" I asked as I walked through the airport, I'd been at my house in North Carolina trying to get some work done for the last three weeks. I have only come out of hiding because Channing finally called and said it was a go for the new shop. He and Jess had done the leg work; it was now my turn to go in and finish it up. We had about two months before the school year got into full swing, and we were walking distance from the local university. It was going to be tough with the time crunch, but I thrived when shit was like this.

I made my way down to the terminal just in time to see the finest chick I'd ever seen in my life. She was standing at the walkway entrance talking to the ticket taker. Even from the side view I could tell she was fine. She had to be at least 5'10, and the color of melted Hershey kisses. She wasn't skinny but not fat, either and she was more than likely a size 16 if I had to guess. Nice thick thighs that slid up to a round ass that more than likely I could sit my drink on. Her stomach had a slight pudge, but her titties had to be a DD cup. Not going to lie. I have a thing about women's necks, they did something to me. And hers screamed for me to just lay my face in between her chin and chest. And oh boy her face, baby girl had to be the finest woman I'd ever seen without a doubt. She must have felt me staring at her when she turned around to pick up her bag because she searched the sitting area. I had to step back a little bit so I wouldn't look like a creep watching her so hard. Baby girl was fine, like drop everything and praise her ever second fine with the slightly pointed chin, full pink lips with her bottom being somewhat larger than the top that led into a small button nose. But it was her eyes hidden behind a pair of two-toned cat-eye rimmed oval glass that got me. My eyes had to be playing tricks on me because it appeared that her eyes were two different colors. You could tell they weren't contacts.

"Chance, did you hear me, man?" Channing all but yelled into the phone. Quickly glancing away from ole girl, I got back into the conversation with my brother. It was business time and I damn sure don't play about my money.

"Yeah, muthafucka, I heard you. Meeting with the interior designer when I get in town, but hell, why can't you do it? Yall are already there, it's stupid that it can't be done by now." Sitting down I waited for my plane to board, I made it a little earlier than I expected to, so I had a few minutes to kill.

"Because I can't." He mumbled into the phone, over the years I had become used to it so when he did it, I understood him completely.

"And why is that nigga?" Pulling out my iPad, I started looking through my emails from potential buyers for a piece I uploaded last night. The twenty new messages I had received made a nigga feel good about his work.

"Why what?" He huffed as if he had an attitude with

me questioning him. I could tell this nigga was about to be on some bull shit with the way he was trying to go around answering my questions.

"Channing stop playing with me, why can't you meet up with the interior designer instead of waiting for me to get into town, it's never been a problem in the past for you or Jess to do this part."I heard him sigh and then I heard his footsteps. And then I heard outdoor noise indicating he had gone outside and away from Jess. "Because nigga the designer is Anlee."

I paused then, looking at my phone screen I hung up and immediately face timed him, and his ass looked stressed. I couldn't even help it I started laughing, out of all the designers in the world he got our oldest brother Choice ex-wife. "Nigga how did Anlee end up here and working for our black asses?"

"Man, Jess set this shit up."

"Does she know it's us?"

"I don't think so, and Jess has no clue about Anlee and Choice."

"I can't believe Anlee was here the entire time, and when Choice finds out ain't no way we can stop that nigga from flying down here and getting in her ass." Leaning back in my seat I looked at my brother and notice he had different reactions. I personally thought it was funny while he continued to sigh. When you mess with people's lives, it always comes back and bites you in the ass. This new shop was about to change our lives in more than one way.

"Aye, man, why I gotta be the one who meets with her?!" I asked as the thought popped into my head.

"Because she liked you better than me, she might only hit you once or twice. Shit with me that girl would only stop hitting me to hit Choice's ass."

"True." Nodding, I got back to looking through my emails. I had a few more minutes before I boarded, then it was a 3-hour flight before I was face to face with my brother's ex-wife.

Clarksville was a small town compared to all the other places we were in. I only noticed how much of a small-town vibe it gave off as I drove from the airport. It had taken me about forty-five minutes to get here, on the drive I passed countless people who waved at me as I drove by. The shocker was how many of them were black, from what Jess said when I called to ask her about it was Clarksville was majority black, and the local college was an HBCU.

Getting out of the car, I looked around at my surrounding, on the left side of the building, set a gym, and the right side a bakery. How we lucked up on this spot is still beyond me, but it was perfect. It seemed we had the best location of the entire block. We sat in the middle of the street, to the left, was a pizza shop, and the right was what looked like an arcade. Directly across the street sat a pet store, a barbershop, a tech store. On the end there was something called The Bar and the other end something called Cigar Club, they didn't look to be in any type of competition both had steady customers. The crowd coming out of the two looked like two completely demographics. I stood next to my rental car looking at the front of our shop, I could imagine a sign hanging over the door and even a small chalkboard sitting in the middle of the walkway showcasing our prices or deals we had going for the day or week.

Heading inside I walked in and stood in what would be considered our lobby, it was a blank canvas, and all I could picture was plants, bright colors, and on the wall, you faced when you walked in a big ass mural of an ocean.

"I'm coming, sorry I was looking around more." I heard

Anlee's voice from the back somewhere before I saw her. When I first met her 12 years ago, I thought Choice had lost his mind when he first started trying to get her attention. We had taken a ride with him over to the local gym, thinking we were going to play a few games of ball, and instead, we followed him to the back where there was a class for steam yoga about to take place. At 6'5, 220 pounds of pure muscle, I just knew Choice black ass wasn't about to do steam yoga, but I was dead ass wrong. He walked right into that hot ass room, unrolled his mat and sat down, and waited. Of course, like the dumb younger brothers that we are Channing and I followed right behind him and did the same thing. We sweated our asses off the entire 90-minute class as we struggled to bend our bodies into some the weirdest positions possible. But we did it, and when we it was over, we watched Choice try and shoot his shot to a girl who sat in the back of the classroom the entire time. She didn't even acknowledge him at first, just kept rolling her mat up and going about her life like she had not heard him. It wasn't until she turned around and damn near bumped into him that she acknowledged his presence, and even that was a quick excuse me, and she took off. It took him months of steam yoga and failed attempts of ignoring him before she agreed to go out on a date with him.

"Hi, I'm Anlee, it's a pleasure- "She stopped talking mid-sentence when she took her eyes off her phone and looked up to see me. I noticed the second she realized who I was, and I realized the second she made her decision that this wasn't going to work. The years had done her more justice than I would have thought. She was still short that would never change, but her body had filled out with grown woman weight that I could tell she managed by working out. She was a shade or two under me on the color spectrum. With a round face, high cheekbones, full lips, small nose, and big full eyes that expressed everything she thought Anlee was and still would be considered drop-dead gorgeous.

"Anlee, please let me explain." Stepping closer, I tried to grab her hand before she could walk past me, but I wasn't quick enough before she sidestepped me, grabbed her purse, and headed out towards the door. "Come on Anlee, he doesn't know you're here. My sister in law set this up. She doesn't know our history."

She didn't even stop walking, with one hand, she flipped me off, and with the other, she pushed open the door and went straight to her car. Literally, she had turned off her hearing. Following behind her, I watched as she got into her car and drove off; her response was a lot better than what I thought it would be. I was sure she was going to curse me out until she was blue in the face; the fact that she walked away was worse. I learned a long time ago that if a woman yelled, screamed, cried, and fussed, she could forgive you. But if she didn't say anything, then she was done and saw no point in fighting a battle she had no intention of being a part of.

"So, what did she say?" Jess said as she looked up from her computer to my brother and me. I wasn't going to say anything; this was not my mess, Channing was supposed to tell her about Anlee and Choice and obviously from her tone and question he hadn't. I looked over at Channing, who suddenly couldn't keep still. His leg was bouncing up and down and he seemed very nervous.. I let out a small laugh, yeah, this nigga had to explain to his woman why the designer she chose for this shop was going to back out.

"Um, hello?" Jess said.

"Well um baby about Anlee." Getting up, Channing

began to pace the floor in front of her. Nigga looked guilty like he was about to tell her she was his ex or something.

"What about her?"

"So, see..." Glancing over at me I remained quiet, like Nah bro. This was all on him. He was going to have to explain it to her and then hope she didn't kick his ass. "Anlee turned off her hearing aid and walked out of the meeting before Chance had an opportunity to talk to her about the design because she used to be married to Choice and she swore off our entire family when they divorced about eight years ago." He basically blurted everything out in one breath, didn't even think about what he said or didn't say. Just laid it all out there on the line and waited for her to explode. Not to mentioned I never said anything to him about Anlee turned off her hearing aid because I wasn't sure if she did or if she was wearing one. She was so good at reading lips that she often did wear it and you couldn't tell plus she wasn't completely deaf. Which was something that not a lot of people knew about her.

Jess looked at me again and then back at Channing, the entire time trying to grasp everything he said before she started laughing uncontrollably. Channing and I looked at each other, and then back at her. We always knew she was little off, but this might be the tipping point.

"Let me get this straight. You mean to tell me that Anlee, the designer is your crazy ass brother ex-wife? Anlee is not just any designer. She's one of the best most reliable designers out here!"

Fixing my shirt, I didn't even take the time out to answer for him because I know Jess well enough to know she wasn't really asking questions but was trying to go through everything in her head. I watched as she struggled with dates and the information. Choice and Anlee happen right after she had left and was over before she had come back. We didn't talk about Anlee because it was still a sore spot for Choice. It was also the longest she had ever been gone at one time, almost a year. A year that she refused to talk about no matter how hard Channing pushed her on the subject.

"Fix it; I don't care how you do it but fix it." She didn't give us a chance to respond; instead, she put on her headphones, and even from across the coffee table, I could hear her music blasting in her ears. Picking up the phone, I went through my emails to find the contact information for Anlee, if Jess wanted her to decorate the shop, then that's what we were going to do.

"What are you doing?" Channing said from the other side of the room. He had gotten so nervous he was rummaging through the fridge to find something to cook, which he only did when he needed to take his mind off something.

"Calling Anlee to fix this." I had hit the call button before I finished my sentence; dealing with Anlee had to be more comfortable than dealing with Jess.

"Hello?" She said after the third ring.

"Anlee its Chance," I rushed out before she could say hello a second time.

click

She hung up, pressing the send button again. I held my breath until she picked up the phone.

"What?!"

The annoyance and aggravation spoke loud and clear in her tone. So much for her being more understanding than Jess, my fucking brothers, and the difficult ass women they dealt with.

FOUR
QUEEN

I was done, finished the last match of my 20-year career. I. Was. Done!

I'm not sure if I'm supposed to be sad or happy, cry or scream, smile or look serious. I had said my final checkmate, shook my last hand and gave my last bow exactly three weeks ago. Now I was sitting on my porch listening to Parker's bossy ass talk my ear off. She talked; I nodded every few minutes and scrolled through my social media timeline. Everyone wished me goodbye from the game. People I had never met, people who had pictures of me at tournaments, people I went to high school, college, and even grade school with. Old teachers even Mrs. Robinson's old ass was on there, opponents, judges, coaches, celebrities, my name, and #Blackgirlmagic and #QueenOfCheckMate took over the internet exactly three weeks ago and hasn't slowed down since. My publicist said I should go on a small press junket and do some interviews, but I was tired. Also, my grandpa told me to sit my ass down, and so that's what I did. I went to the beach, got some sun.. I didn't have anything to worry about, and now I was bored.

"Have you talked to Anlee?" Leaning against the bottom step of my porch, I watched as my neighbors went about their lives. From the old lady Ms. Morris next door pulling weeds out her garden to older man, Mr. Curtis half sleep on his porch swing. I lived on a mostly quiet block; it would be perfect if it wasn't for Mr. and Mrs. Jennings and their constant fighting over him cheating.

"Yeah, she's been working on some project for a tattoo shop. We are going to The Bar later; you are coming. My parents came and got Harlem this morning, so I'm kid-free." She said as she swatted at a bug that was near her.

"I gotta choice?"

"Nope, we're all going out to celebrate."

"Celebrate what?"

"Your retirement, new job, random Saturday hell I don't know. We are just going to have a good time, and before you start up, understand we are going to get drunk, be loud, and possibly find you some new dick because if I see Dr. Doctor smiling one more damn time when I walk through the hospital I'm going to scream."

"Who the hell is Dr. Doctor?" Laughing I waited for her to answer my question, I pretty much know who she is talking about since I've only been with two men in the last five years, but hearing her calling him by some other name killed me.

"You know the dentist that you've been screwing the last two years that likes to tell people he's a doctor." She said as she looked at me like I was a permanent rider of the short bus.

"That's because he is."

"He's a damn dentist." She said as she rolled her eyes, making her way to the tire swing I had installed for both Kory and Harlem.

"That means he's a doctor."

"It's a difference; trust me."

"I haven't spoken to him in a while, so if he's walking around smiling, It has nothing to do with me."

"If we were only so lucky, that fool has been counting down the days until you came home. Don't be surprised if he pops up on you soon." Instead of sitting on it correctly, I watched as she climbed up the rope a little so she could place her feet into the opening and swing standing up.

Standing, I couldn't help but laugh more at her. She knew the man was a doctor, and even though he went to dental school instead of medical, she still should give him his props, but she never did. Hell no one did, they always reminded him that he was just a dentist when he corrected people by adding the Dr. part to his name. He was a little compulsive with it, which is why he never made it past a fuck buddy. He couldn't pass my rule of being true to yourself and not worrying about what other people thought of you.

"Whatever that man is not worried about me. He has other stuff to do than worry about me."

"Mark my words, he's going to bring his nerdy ass around here wanting some. When he does call, make sure you call me so I can turn him down for you. What did you ever see in him in the first place is beyond me?" She said as she climbed right back down off the swing to follow behind me.

"He's nice."

"He's boring and safe, but anyway, are you coming or not?

"What time should I be ready?" I asked as we walked to the garage where she had parked her car. The giant F150 dwarfed my small sports car, making my three-car garage seem smaller than it was. After starting her truck, she rolled down the window and put on her sunglasses.

"I'll be back around 8:30; I already know I'm going to have to argue with you about putting on some sexy clothes."

"You could just not and let me wear what I want," I said, crossing my arms over my chest.

"Or you could just let me do what I do best and not argue with me. Oh, and you will not be wearing orange!" She yelled as she backed down the driveway rolling up her window before I had a chance to respond. After closing the door, I headed towards my room. She will be back by 8:30, which meant I had time to take a quick nap, and that's exactly what I planned on doing.

The music was too loud, it smelled like weed and incense, and I know for a fact we were going to have a good ass time. It was only Parker, Anlee and I, our friend Cooper was supposed to meet us but was out of town due to a family function. Her family was huge and always found a reason to get together, and with her job being dangerous, she made sure to try to show up to everything she could. She'd been a cop for a few years and had just been promoted to the Narcotics division while I was away, and she was more than excited and ready to start. We planned to get together when she got back in town to celebrate.

We'd only been here for about twenty minutes, and I was already ready to go home. When Parker pulled back up at exactly 8:30 with a duffle bag and a smirk on her face, I knew I was in for a long night. Luckily for me, the outfit in the duffle bag wasn't for me. The orange romper with khaki-colored booties Parker picked out for me to wear from my closet looked great against my dark skin, my sister locs had been semi styled by Anlee since they'd been pulled back into a ponytail for a few weeks while on the road. Even though she said no orange it's exactly what she pulled out, Parker credited the entire look to her. To justify her use of orange, she changed the name of it and called it Tiger. The truth was the shit was dark orange, no matter how she tried to spin it. Tonight I didn't even wear my contacts, so I had this sexy schoolgirl look going on also. I had heterochromia iridium, and I hated for people to stare once they realized I had one grey eye and one blue.

"Shit ma' you're the finest woman I have ever seen, please tell me you don't have a man." The deep baritone voice startled me but not in a good way; it was more out of annoyance than anything else. I hate men who called women "Ma" like a little boy if you don't sit the hell down with that. I am not, nor do I plan on being someone's mother, so calling me "ma" was not the way to get or keep my attention. But with the slim prospects of quality men here, I said a quick prayer that he wasn't attractive because hurting his feels would be that much harder to do. Turning, I had to step back and look up slightly; I was tall for a woman standing at 5'11, and with 6-inch heels on, I stared at the skinny, pimply face kid standing in front. His face immediately made me turn sour. He was a baby. Eventually, he could have potential, but I don't date younger men, especially ones who still had titty milk on their breath.

"Little boy, that ride will have you crying to your mama and begging your daddy to tell you it's going to be okay," Parker said from beside me, her dark brown eyes glowed under the lights as she held in her laughter.

"It's true, son, go away before she hurts your feelings," Anlee said from the other side of me. She didn't hide her laughter, couldn't if she wanted to. She always got a kick out of watching younger men try to pick one of us up. She said their confidence was beyond their years, even if their nuts hadn't dropped, and they weren't done with puberty.

"Sweetie, go on. I'm not interested." Smiling softly at him, I watched as he walked away, his pride still intact, head even high. Little baby Smoove walked right up to the next woman and took his shot; he didn't even give me another thought. Me turning him down did nothing to his confidence or intention of getting a woman's full attention for the night.

"Queen, just admit to them your pussy is amazing, and if they aren't real men, they'll run away," Parker said in between sips of whatever she had ordered, more than likely tequila. She always drank tequila, had since she watched that TV show Grey's and the main characters sat in a bar drinking it. She said they looked like they were having fun, and if tequila did that for them, then maybe she should try it. That was ten years ago, and it was still her go-to drink.

"What if they don't back down?" Looking over the drink menu, I placed my order on the screen in front of me and waited for them to answer.

"If he doesn't run, it means one of two things; he thinks he can handle you." Anlee started to answer as she waved at different people who passed by us. Some I knew but most of them I didn't. More than likely, they were clients of hers. With her being one of the few interior designers in the area who was worth a damn, she was always busy with new and returning clients. So, when we went out, people always spoke.

"Or he knows he can, which will leave your pussy craving him like a junky looking for his next fix. Personally, I vote yes for him if that means you don't have to deal with Dr. Doctor anymore." Fixing her top, Parker barely glanced at me. Her dislike for Joshua was evident in the way she spoke about him. The day after she introduced us, she told me she regretted it, his behavior and attitude immediately turned sour towards her and any other person I dealt with. When I brought it up to him, he had denied it, saying that they were jealous of our relationship. That was another reason we hadn't progressed past fuck buddies, my support system knew and voiced I deserved better. When I told them I chose to have a sexual relationship with him, they simply told me to supply my condoms because he seemed like the type that would try and get me pregnant to keep me around.

"I second that," Anlee said from her seat, quickly turning to her, I was a little shocked. She never really gave her opinion on who I did or didn't deal with. She always said she was our support, not our mama, so she didn't give her opinion on matters that didn't involve her.

"You too?" I sighed.

"Sorry, sis, but I'm beyond tired of seeing Dr. Doctors face. He's kind of annoying. Plus, he has three qualities on that long-ass list you have regarding dating. No reason to waste your time on someone you're eventually going to get bored with." Shrugging, she didn't look sorry about telling me how she felt. If they were all voicing their opinion on our lack, then luster sexual relationship, it was time to give it a second thought. If I needed a nut that bad, some toys could help me out with that. Truth be told, I only dealt with him this long because he was easily accessible when I was in town. As we talked about what was going on, they caught me up on their lives; I couldn't help but look around the room; I could feel someone's eyes on me. I just couldn't figure out who it was.

"What is up with everyone being against my list?" I asked once I turned back around. They had known about the list for years and hardly brought it up. Maybe I was paranoid because of the conversation I had with my mother less than a month ago, but it felt like everyone was bringing it up now.

"Nothing is wrong with it. It's just a damn list is all. You're supposed to let things flow. Catch his vibe and ride that bitch." Anlee said as she readjusted in her seat. Her bangles that she wore around her right wrist clanked together as she waved at me.

"And if you are going to ride the vibe for a little, you may as well ride his dick," Parker said as she smiled brightly and did a little shimmy in her seat.

FIVE
CHANCE

After a long day at the shop, putting the final touches on the ocean mural that would take up a much larger space than I originally planned, I needed to relax. So, when Jess mentioned going to the bar, I jumped at the opportunity to see what this place had to offer. It was small, held maybe a hundred people but it was nice. With a DJ giving a 90's and today's music in heavy rotation, it gave you the vibe of grown and sexy. When you looked into the crowd, you could see the younger grown here too. They weren't out of control, ready to knuck if you buck type of crowd. They looked like they were just here to have a good time, which I was okay with.

"Man, I can't believe we open up in a few days. You ready?" Damn near dropping back in his seat, Channing looked like he was about to sweat through his shirt. He and Jess had been on the dance floor for the last 2 hours. They danced to damn near every song that came on. I could tell from the stupid grin on his face that they were in a good place. Now how long that lasted was entirely up in the air.

Sometimes she stayed around for months, and other times it was weeks.

"Hell yeah." Taking a sip of my beer, I continued watching a group of women I noticed when they first walked in for the last thirty minutes talked amongst their selves.

"What are you looking at, or should I say who?" He'd damn near chugged his entire glass of water down right after he asked me. Peering over at him quickly, then to the bar, I watched as Jess made her way over with three drinks in her hands. Her all black parachute jumpsuit had nigga's moving out her way to get a better look at her, but she never took o eyes off my brother.

"Just enjoying the scenery is all. This place has a nice vibe." Taking the drinks out of Jess's hands, I sat them down on the table. "Thank you, sis."

"No problem, you got first round it wasn't even questioned if we were going to get the next one." She said as she drank her water just as quickly as Channing had.

"I'm not going to lie. I was surprised as hell when I walked in."

"Yeah, us too when we decided to come last week. From what Jess found out from Anlee, the DJ and bartender are sisters and own it." Kissing Jess on the cheek, he leaned back in his chair and pulled her down into his lap. She willingly sat down and seemed to be taking in the room, as well. Jess was always up for supporting black women and tried to as much as possible. She always insisted on using as many black-owned businesses as much as she could. She followed thousands on social media, and whenever we were looking for someone new, she would get on there, announce it, and before we knew it, she would have numbers to different businesses and setting up meetings. She told us that's how she found Anlee, just got on there and asked, and someone mentioned her.

"Oh, look babe Anlee is here, we should go say hello." Nodding her head in the direction of the table I had been watching, I turned to play it off like I didn't know she was there. But it wasn't her I had been watching; it was the woman in the orange romper that I noticed when they first walked in. It was the chick from the airport a few weeks back. At first, I wasn't so sure because I could only see the side of her face, but once she turned around and looked around the room as if she could feel someone watching her, I knew for sure it was her. It was just my luck; she couldn't see me in the dark corner. But it didn't matter, I knew she was here, and she knew Anlee. I'd find out all the necessary information I needed to know before I introduced myself to her.

"Nah baby, let her be. She deals with us enough. We will see her Monday. You already know she doesn't like Chance and I that much as it is." Moving her to a different leg, Channing tried to play it cool.

"Speak for yourself nigga; she likes me. You on the other hand? I'm pretty sure she's going to knock your ass out when she gets an opportunity." I said after I drank some of my jack and coke. I hid my smile behind my drink as Channing shot me a killer look.

"What the hell did you do to that woman? She's nice as hell." Leaning back against him, Jess tilted her head to get a better look at him as she waited for his explanation. Grinning harder, I watched as he stammered around her question. He'd never admit that he was the reason for their divorce at least not to anyone else. Anlee looked up from her phone as if she knew we were talking about her and gave Jess and I a small smile and wave, but when she made eye contact with Channing, her smiled dropped, and she signed *"Fuck you"* to him. Her entire table turned and looked in our direction, trying to figure out who she was talking to.Jess and I doubled over in laughter.

"Told you nigga, she hates yo ass, not us." I said while trying to pull myself together.

I TURNED the music as loud as I could. I sat in the back office and worked on our social media pages. We have been promoting our new shop on the radio and social media for a few months now. We hooked up with a few bloggers and podcasters in the area, and we did a few interviews to make our presence known. I'd talked Channing into doing raffle give away for a free tattoo; he only agreed after we set the price for $200 or less. So far, we'd sold almost two grand in raffle tickets, so we had more than covered the price of the tattoo and our time. Turning my attention away from the tattoo for a little, I pulled up a new tab for my internet on my phone. I pulled up Anlee's social media page and browsed through her post. I asked her about her friend a few days ago after we saw them at the bar and she flat out told me to get some guts and find out on my own. She'd wouldn't even tell me her name. So, I decided to go the new age route and do a little social media peep work. I found not a damn thing. Anlee had absolutely no pictures of the woman on any of her pages that I could tell. How women were able to play an FBI agent and find out everything they wanted to know about someone on social media was beyond me. Now granted I was only looking at her business pages because she declined all my friend request on her personal pages, and she'd sworn Jess to secrecy. Jess wasn't telling us because we wouldn't tell her what Channing did to have her hate him so much. So, I was stuck waiting to see if I would run into her again around town.

When my phone dinged with a text from Channing asking me to meet him back at the bar for lunch, I jumped at the opportunity. I was hungry, and I wasn't getting any work done, so why not? Please, I wanted to see the vibe of this place in the daytime. Jess had sworn by the food when we were out the other night, but I wasn't someone who played about their food, so I passed. If their drinks were good, then I hoped their food was as well because I could see myself going back there for the night vibe again.

SIX
QUEEN

"You ever been so high you thought the ceiling was falling in on you?" I asked as we sat around waiting after Kin had taken our order. We were meeting up for our weekly lunch date that we had whenever all of us were in town at the same time and not busy working.

"What?" Everyone asked at the same time. Parker looked damn near giddy with excitement as she hopped up and down in her seat. Her eyes bright with question and smile, taking up damn near her entire face. Anlee looked confused, and Cooper, who had gotten back in town earlier today, looked ready to arrest us all if we said the wrong thing.

"It's a legitimate question that I want the answer to." Shrugging I lean back in my seat to get more comfortable. We were sitting at the bar so we could hold a conversation with Kin too as she worked.

"Why?" Parker said, she was smiling at us like she was up to something. "You wanna get high? Please tell me you do; I've been waiting to get you high since I met you." Parker was already digging in her bag before she finished her sentence. Knowing her she had a blunt or edible in her purse just for a moment like this. Her lion's mane as she likes to call it because that's what it looked like moved freely around her round face as she dug away.

, "I know there is no damn way you have something in your bag, and I'm sitting right here." Cooper whispered from the other side of Anlee. Cooper was as straight-laced as they came, so this scene was not for her. Plus, when she and Parker got around each other, it was nonstop bickering. They reminded me of sisters who were making up for lost time with all the arguing they did. As annoying as they were with each other, they always had each other's back.

"I don't have anything hardcore. I do have a joint or two, or five. It's harmless I'm telling you. Like one-time bitch, I ate like three edibles I had in my purse that I forgot about for maybe three months. I don't know why I ate them, but I did. I was so high I called my mom from a closet and told her the dark had abducted me. After her and my dad talked me into opening the door to my bedroom that was in their house, by the way.I knew I had to leave that shit alone." Parker said, trying not to laugh at herself while explaining to everyone at the table. We all knew she was crazy but sometimes we just had to sit back and just laugh at her.

"But your parents live almost 3 hours away, how the fuck did you get to their house?" Anlee asked, trying not to laugh.. We all wanted to, but she asked a question we all needed the answers too.

"Don't know, don't even care. I just knew after that day I had to leave the shit alone. So now I partake in the natural herbs and only the herbs." Parker laughed as she tried to eat the rest of her salad. "My mom had me promise, and yall know how I am when I promise her something."

"Was this before or after Harlem?" Cooper asked as she shook her head.

"Literally the week before, the next day, I prayed for something to change my ways, and the phone call came on that Saturday that her mom wanted to give her up. So, I took that as my sign." She said, playing off the impact of taking in a younger sibling by her father that she knew nothing about. It was one of the layers of Parker that people didn't know about. She let people think what they wanted about her and saw no reason to correct them.

"Next thing on my list of change is to get high. Not anything crazy just a simple high." I said to them as they all looked at me like I was crazy again.

"We're getting high!" Parker all but yelled, causing people at the surrounding tables to look at us.

"I'm taking you to jail," Cooper said, looking around the room.

"I don't care what we do at this point," Anlee said as she took a sip of her drink and dismissively shrugged her shoulders.

"You need dick, and it's the only reason why you are as grouchy as you are right now." Sitting our food down in front of us, Kin said, and we all agreed. Anlee was grouchy had been for the last few weeks, and none of us knew why. So, we went with the logical reason, she was horny, and her toys weren't doing it for her anymore.

"I don't need dick." She damn near rolled her eyes into the back of her head. She was trying to keep her attitude in check so we wouldn't be proving her wrong.

"I'm pretty sure you do. I mean you're, moody, short-tempered, quick to go off on someone. Plus, I'm pretty sure the other day you turned off your hearing aid in the middle of our conversation because you got upset." Parker said as she counted off each incident on a finger.

"Oh, and you flipped that guy off the other day and signed fuck you." Jumping into the conversation, I couldn't help but laugh as she rolled her eyes once again.

"And that love is not like you. Kin or Cooper, yes, but you? No." Parker said as she pointed at Kin and Cooper who absently nodded their head in agreement.

"Which by the way Parker had to call and tell me about and you know how she gets when she's telling a story. For a possible five-minute conversation, it was twenty because she was laughing so hard." Cooper said as she pushed her hair out her face.Up until about a year ago, she had always worn braids, then one day, she came over, and her hair was cut into a cute asymmetrical bob. She said it was to much work and cut it into a fade which lasted a few months.She is now allowing the top to grow out while the sides were still in a taper fade.

"So, we've come to the conclusion that you need dick." Kin said as she came back around the bar and prepared to make our drinks. Her sister Rae was making her way back inside from the storage room with a case of wine and beer on a dolly.

"You ever think I could just be having a frustrating moment in my life and need my friends to help me work through it?"

"Nope." We all answered in unison, which caused all of us, including Anlee, to laugh. We weren't being mean when we answered. Anlee was usually the one we were least worried about. She lived a low-key life, she owned her own company and enjoyed her free time by traveling, and when she had a rough patch, she said so. She was transparent with her emotions, and we respected her for it. So, the fact that she hadn't said anything told us that she was full of shit.

"Fine, but I don't mostly need dick. I am lonely, though; I need companionship; I crave it." Throwing her hands up dramatically, we once again started laughing at her. Even though we laughed we knew she wasn't joking, Anlee's love language is physical touch. When she was in a relationship, she thrived off it, she said, and we believed it made her a better person. It calmed her soul.

"If that was your problem, all you had to do was make a call; we all know he would've come running." A voice said from behind us, quickly, we all turned around to see two of the finest men in the world standing behind us. They had to be two of the finest men I'd ever seen in my life. Both a milk chocolate color, around 6'4, short taper fade haircuts that led to short but full beards wrapped around kissable plump lips. Both their noses were slightly cocked noses, dark eyes, and full eyebrows. They wore t-shirts, one red and the other grey and black cargo shorts. The one in red wore red and black Nike air max's, and the one in grey wore grey chucks, which were my favorite type of shoes, so points for him. If I saw them in the street, I would've done a double-take.

"Um, excuse us, but do we know you?" Parker said from her chair, her attitude waiting to shine through if they said the wrong thing. As goofy as she was, her protective instincts kicked in quickly. Cooper was right next to her, ready for whatever and whoever.

"Nah, we don't know yall, but we know her." The one in the red said, from the look of anger on Anlee's face, we all knew he wasn't lying. "I'm Channing, and this is my brother, Chance. We own the new tattoo shop down the way." Red shirt who we now know as Channing said, the entire time he never took his eyes off Anlee. His look wasn't sexual; if anything, it had a hint of fear and hope in it.

"So how yall know Anlee?" Kin said from her spot behind the bar.I almost forgot she was there. She didn't do confrontation very well. In most cases, she avoided it, but her sister Rae' was the polar opposite and was always down to fight.

"She's our sister in law; she's married to our oldest brother Choice." Channing said causing us to turn an look at Anlee. She turned to face the bar and had begun eating her food.

"Anlee tell these men they have you confused." Looking over, I waited for her to respond to Parker's statement, but she didn't.

"She turned off her hearing aid. She has a tendency to do that when he starts talking." Shaking his head, Chance looked over at Anlee for a quick second before making eye contact with me. His lop-sided smile made me smile back at him.I didn't miss how he scanned me from head to toe, and when his eyes reached mine, he slowly licked his lips. If their other brother looked anything like them how the hell did, she just walk away from him and not come running back.

"Hi, I'm Chance." Stepping forward, it seemed like he blocked everything around us. His body heat making me want to move closer to him. And his smell? My pussy immediately woke up and got wet.

"I'm Queen." Shaking his hand, I smiled back at him. Yeah, Anlee had some damn explaining to do. Where the hell had these brothers been at this entire time?

SEVEN
CHANCE

Her name is Queen.When we walked into the bar, I noticed her sitting there with her friends and decided before either one of them left I would introduce myself. We hadn't intentionally overheard what they were talking about, we were on our way to a table, and of course, Channing had to open his mouth and say something. That was one of the reasons why Anlee didn't like him, he talked to damn much, especially about something he had no business running his mouth about. It was also why Choice and Anlee had broken up years ago. He was in his feelings about Jess leaving, and when Choice told us how he and Anlee had gotten into it, and she threatens to leave him, Channing told him to pack her bags for her. Why he listened to Channing was something I could never figure out. Anlee had taken one look at her bags sitting by the front door when she had come home from work and Channing's smug face as he sat on the couch she didn't say anything just picked up her shit and walked out. When Choice was about to run behind her, Channing told him to let her go and that she would be back. She didn't have any family that we knew of, so it wasn't likely she would stay gone for long. That had been the last time we saw her because she didn't come back. It took him a few years, and a lot of ass whooping's to forgive Channing for running his mouth. But he always took responsibility for his actions; he said he had done the one thing he said he would never do. He gave up on the woman who had come into his life and helped him become a better man. We did not know they were married until he received the divorce papers in the mail. They were only together for about eight months.

"I called Choice and told him she was here."

I looked up from my spot on the floor since I knew I had heard him wrong. There was no way he called our brother and told him after we both had told Anlee that we would not. It had been a few hours since he ran his mouth at the restaurant and outed Anlee. After I introduced myself to Queen, we made our exit but not before I saw the tear drop down her face.

"Nigga are you trying to make her hate you? Like why the fuck would you do that?"

"Because he deserves to know." Turning on the TV, he plopped down on my couch after grabbing the Xbox controller.

"He deserves to know?! Nigga did you forget he packed her shit and had it sitting by the door when she got home from work?" Putting my hand over the sensor so he couldn't connect to the system, I waited for him to respond. Yeah, I know it was childish, and I'd done it my entire childhood when my brothers tried to change the channel, but I needed all his attention on our conversation.

"Yeah, I remember, I was there when he did it."

"Of course, you were there when he did it; it was your fucking idea. She deserved to be happy then! And she deserves to be happy now! To not be put in a situation that she has to move different in her comfort zone like she's the one in the wrong." Getting up off the floor, I damn near yelled at the top of my lungs. Why couldn't he see that what he was doing was fucked up? Anlee asked us damn near begged us not to tell him she was here. She said she was at peace with everything when we tried to explain that it wasn't our intention to change her life in any way , shape, or form. But it was like she didn't believe us, and dumb ass Channing had proved her right. It was like he hadn't heard a damn word she said to us. "Man go home, you and your dumb ass behavior is giving me a headache, lock the door on your way out."

"I'm trying to fix this shit." He said, jumping up off the couch, throwing his hands up in the air, trying to act surprised to the fact I was putting him out for some stupid shit he had done. He acted like the youngest sometimes; the dumb shit was starting to get old and fast.

"Nah nigga you not fixing shit this way! She ain't Jess; she told that nigga from jump to not throw her away. If he couldn't handle it, then he should have said that. They petty little argument could have been fixed.The first year of marriage is the hardest. We know that! Now granted, we didn't know they were married, but we knew it would've eventually got there. They had all the odd's stacked against them anyway because they barely knew each other, so the shit was fresh as hell on all levels. But Choice dumb ass listened to you and your dumb ass logic of letting her go. And where did that get him nigga?" I said, I turned around so fast to confront his dumb ass. I'm pretty sure I had whiplash. I knew for whatever reason back then he'd talked Choice into packing her stuff, it was jealousy. He was jealous that Choice had found someone who loved him with everything in her. Anlee didn't want anything from him, but his love, and he'd given it to her in a short amount of time. Yeah, he was jealous of something that he wasn't and still isn't getting from Jess. A full no holds bar commitment.

"Fuck man you so fucking stupid sometimes! What works in your relationship ain't going to work in every relationship you know that shit." I said to him, why couldn't he figure that shit out was beyond me.

"Well he's going to be here by night fall."Channing said as if he hadn't heard anything I'd said to him.

"And I hope she runs both you niggas over." Sighing I walked away, he wasn't going to get it. I just hoped Choice would listen to reason before he went chasing after her.

WHEN I HEARD YELLING in front of the tattoo shop two days later, I knew Choice hadn't listened to anything I said when he came into town. He slept for a few hours and had been on the hunt looking for Anlee since. I sent her a text letting her know he was in town just so she wouldn't be blindsided. Her reply was a simple okay, and that was it. From the sound coming from the front, it seemed like her luck had run out. Making my way to the front, I watched as a pissed off Anlee was being held back by an amused Queen. Choice stood in front of her and saying nothing. If it weren't for the tears running down Anlee's face, this would be considered funny.

"You don't get to come here! You don't get to come and fuck my life up because you want to. It's been years Choice, years! Your stupid ass brother ran his fucking mouth after I told him not to, and here you come running back full steam ahead. Do you remember our last conversation? Huh?! I know you do because it still plays over and over in my head daily!" She stopped yelling; her voice was barely above a whisper as if she was about to tell him the secrets of the universe. "You packed my shit, told me to bounce. Now you want to come back in here and act like shit did happen? Like we don't have a history and it's got a fucked-up ending? Now, this time I'm telling you no and I'm meaning it with everything in me." Queen slowly let her go and she walked out the shop. Her head down, shoulders slumped, she didn't look back or wait for her friend. It was like she just gave up, like there was no more fight left in her.

"I'm going to fight for her. Prove that I need her just like she needs me." Choice said to Queen, she simply just stared at him. As if she was unimpressed by what he had said.

"Look, I don't know you. Never heard of you before your brothers mentioned your name, but I know her. And from what she has told me over the last few days, you fucked up, and that woman that just walked out that door ain't the type to give second chances. I don't know what she was like before but I'm telling you now you have no clue what you're about to get yourself into." Queen said while shaking her head; she headed out the door. "And I'll be honest, I'm not even rooting for you because I know she deserves the best thing the world has to offer her." She threw over her shoulder right before she walked completely out.

"Told yo dumb ass not to listen to Channing. Now look at you." I left him standing there as I headed out the door right behind Queen.

EIGHT
QUEEN

Glancing down again on my phone, I couldn't help but smile at the fact my grandparents were Face timing me. Swiping to answer, I waited to hear my grandfather try to get his baring's together before he said hello.

"Queen shit hold on, I almost got it figured out this time." Grandpa looked good at 76. He looked to be in his early 60's. His hair had the salt and pepper thing going, barely any wrinkles, and still worked out every day. He once told me he would rather work out then eat my Granny's food. As much as we loved her, we couldn't tolerate her cooking. That was one skill she didn't get from her southern roots.When we said she burned food we meant literally she burnt that shit up. She had maybe two meals she could barely scrap together. Growing up grandpa cooked all the meals, or they had a chef come in weekly and prepare all their meals for them. "Girl look at you! You are looking like yo mama! How are you?"

"I'm good, Grandpa! How are you?" I could see my grandmother in the back, rolling her eyes like she always did once we were on the phone. We talked every other day, almost always on Face time, and she couldn't figure out why it still took him a few minutes to figure out how to work the phone. "Hey back there stop rolling your eyes at my Grandpa!" I couldn't help but laugh more when granny flipped me off; she was so childish.

"Oh, don't pay her any mind Queen she's just mad I put her in time out for the week." Grandpa waved Granny off and focused back on me. "How are you likin' retirement?" They were the only grandparents I had left, my dad's father died not too long after his wife died in the late '90.s. Even though they owned their own art gallery and were busy, they were always there for us. When I had a tournament, and I needed someone to go with me because my mom couldn't just take off. During my early years, my grandparents had decided to allow my parents to be more active in the galleries. So instead of my parents being at everything, they went. They had my back through it all, and I do mean it all. From my first heartbreak, when I got my period, and when even after Granny sat me down and told me about the birds and the bees. I was traumatized by the entire thought process of some boy sticking his penis in my vagina. They were my rock. I can't even say "were" because that made it seem like past tense. They are still my rock. Even if they were a little crazy, they were meant for each other. When I asked them why they stopped their lives for us. They said it was their job as grandparents to do everything that our parents couldn't. And if that meant they spent their time with us running from tournament to tournament then so be it. Granny always said it was our parent's turns to run the business long before we all found our niche in life; we just happen to see what we loved at an early age. At times I think my granny loved the fact she was the one who ran me around town and the country.

She said that I could get away from the tense relationship my mother and I developed wasn't healthy and she really couldn't figure out why she acted the way that she did because she raised all of us the same way. She just treated some of her children better than others. Again, I suppose it's the money thing. Extra zeroes in your bank account can change you. I respected their hustle when it came to dominating in the Art world. There weren't too many black people making a name for themselves in it.I respected them more than anything because they had been the ones who made sure we were never put on the back burner for anyone else in the world. They were my loudest supporters and would quickly go off on anyone who thought it would be a good idea to try and make me feel less worthy of the recognition and praise I received while playing.

"Time out?" I was confused; Granny was a grown-ass woman; she didn't have any bad habits that I knew of. She hated shopping ever since they had moved back to the south, so all she did was garden. Which in all honesty she wasn't to great at either; she did not have a green thumb and killed pretty much everything she touched.We loved her none the less, and we all supported her new venture.

"Yeah, Queen time out, this old fool took the dick from me for two weeks cause he selfish." Oh, hell no, I didn't need to know this, I didn't give two shits about my grandparent's sex life. In fact, in my opinion, it was nonexistent, and partly I was jealous that at their age, they still had a very active sex life. I'm guessing my facial expression must have shown my disapproval because both couldn't stop laughing. While I don't find shit funny, I'm glad they do because I wasn't having it. "And on that note, I love you; I'll talk to you all soon." And I hung up the phone. Nope, grandparents and sex don't mix in my book. I didn't need that visual in my head.

"I called Anlee almost a dozen times to make sure she was okay. This town isn't big, so you know I've been looking for your face in the crowd every time I go places." Looking up I watched as Chance made his way towards my porch; he was right. We lived in a small town, so he eventually walking by my house would happen no matter. He looked damn good; his dark caramel skin tone looked amazing in the sun. I could get a better look at his face now too and the girls were right, he is to fine to pass up. He was taller than me, which is good because I couldn't stand a man being shorter than me.I bet money on it. He had been down to Ernie's getting a fresh cut because his line was sharp. High cheekbones, slightly pointed chin, thick lashes, and the darkest set of eyes I'd ever seen. It was his swag as he walked towards me that made me sit up a little higher; he wasn't a southern boy.

"I haven't been hiding." Leaning back, I watched as he sat down on my bottom step, dude didn't care one bit about if I wanted his company or not. "Yeah sure, have a seat." Sarcasm was my go-to when I didn't know what else to say or do.

"But you still jetted like the police wanted you, and you heard sirens."

"I didn't! I went after Anlee to make sure she was okay. Unlike you, I know where she lives, and she answered the phone for me when I called. I've only been home for about thirty minutes. I sat with her while she calmed down and eventually fell asleep. Whatever your brother has planned better be good because she has no interest in hearing what he has to say or dealing with him period." He turned slightly to look at me.He was sizing me up, not in a threatening way.

More so, he was trying to figure me out, what was real, what was fake. The eyes? Obviously, they always went for the eyes. That's usually why I wore colored contacts, I got too many questions about them, it was annoying after a while. "Their real, the eyes are real. I have Heterochromia iridium." I said as he finally made eye contact with me. The way his eyes roamed my body sent tingles right down to my pussy. I had to cross my legs because as quickly as I got wet he'd be able to see the wet spot in the crotch of my pants.

"I've heard of that before, that's what Ashton Kutcher's wife has right?" Nodding, he watched me for a second then turned back towards the street. I lived in a quiet neighborhood, not too far from campus and downtown. I'd bought the house three years ago when the market crashed at a steal, hadn't regretted it yet. "Never knew black people could have it too."

"It's a genetic thing. My grandmother has it too."

"I honestly never saw it before in person. Even ol' boys wife wears contacts. The only reason I know about her is that my little sister's obsessed with her."

"Besides my granny, a cousin of mine and Mila', that's his wife's name just so you know, I've never seen anyone else with it. It took me years to get comfortable enough with it to look people in their eyes when I talk to them. Now when I'm not in the mood to deal with people staring, or I know I'll be around a lot of people I've never met, I wear contacts." I said as I pushed my favorite pair of glasses up on my face.Leaning back on the swing I watched as him as he watched Mrs. Jennings my next-door neighbor as she sat her husband's clothes on the curb. He must be cheating again; every few months, they did this. They would be entertainment for the next few days.

"But you know my offer still stands, right?" Glancing

over he watched me for a second then turned back towards Mrs. Jennings. He never seemed to look at me for longer than a second or two. And I only noticed that because I hadn't stopped staring at him.

"What offer?" Maybe I had blanked out for a second because I don't remember him offering me anything.

"In my head, the first time I saw you. I asked you out on a date; it's not my fault you didn't hear me."

Laughing I got up from my seat, yeah, he was funny, I loved a funny man."Then I gave you my answer the same way, not fault you didn't hear me."

"Touché'. You leaving me out here?" He sounded shocked at the thought. I not only turned him down in his head, but I was also walking away from him again.

"You see that car coming?" I pointed out the red Honda making its way down the street. "That's Mr. Jennings, the husband of the woman sitting clothes on the curb. I'm going to get me some popcorn; this is going to be funny."

"You see it, Queen?!" Mrs. Morris, my other neighbor, said as she made her way back onto her porch.

"Yes, ma'am, I'm getting ready to grab me a snack, and I'm coming right back out," I yelled over to her as she made herself comfortable on her porch swing.

"This a regular thing for yall?" I'd forgotten he was still there, glancing over my shoulder I shrugged and headed into the house.

"You can stay if you'd like, more than likely you'll get a better show than anything on TV."

When I came back, he'd gotten comfortable on the swing, gesturing for him to move down. He grabbed the popcorn from my hands just as Mrs. Morris came out the house with a bat and headed towards her husband's car.

"Well, shit looks like she's pissed." He said as he

adjusted his black fitted Royal's baseball cap. He looked good in a pair of black cargo shorts, blue fitted tee and black retro Jordan's. I couldn't help but notice his entire right side of his body from the bottom of his ear all the way down to his shoe top was covered in tattoos. I could not help but wonder how many other tattoos he has.

"I bet you twenty dollars. She hits him with that bat again." Mrs. Morris yelled over from her porch. We'd developed a friendship over the last few years. She watched my house while I was out of town and when I was home, we sat on the porch and caught up on the news around town. At eighty-two, she still had a life to live but needed to slow down. And that's where I came in. She and her friends held a bingo game three times a week at the local community center and gossiped. When she wasn't there, she was at the park walking the trails to stay in shape. About a year ago she had fallen while out and was in the hospital. She called me daily to complain about the staff. After that, we agreed to our porch meetings, and once a week, we had dinner together.

"Fifty says he cries." I said back to her.

"Deal."

"HOW'D you know he would cry?" Laughing, Chance wiped his mouth with his napkin. We'd sat outside for nearly an hour listening as the Jennings's argued. Eventually Mr. Jennings started to cry, and Mrs. Jennings forgave him.

"It's what they do. He cheats, she gets pissed, puts his stuff out, he comes home, she forgives him and repeats. Since I've lived here, it's been the same way. It's how Mrs.

Morris and I became friends." Shrugging, I picked over my salad with my fork as we talked. We now sat back at Blue's Bar, eating an early dinner. It seemed like neither one of us wanted to be away from the other, the conversation flowed smoothly. The chemistry was there even the sexual chemistry was making itself known.

"So, what do you do for a living?" He asked as he set further back in his seat. His dark eyes watching me closely.

"I recently retired from chess, and in about three weeks, I will be a third-grade teacher."

"Retired from chess? Like you were a professional chess player, or you just hustled little kids for their lunch money?" Smiling he asked me.

"Professionally. I've been playing since I was in the second grade, but only competing for money when I turned 16."

"Really?" He said I could tell from his tone and facial expression he was confused. There weren't too many professional players in the US, and there were even fewer women, an even smaller amount was black, and to be honest, I've only met three other black women in the game.

"Yeah, let me see your phone. I can prove it to you." I said as I wiped my hands on with a napkin. It was all too often I had to explain what I did to someone. As soon as I told what I did, their interest became minimal. So, for him to genuinely seem interested, it was like a breath of fresh air.

He handed me his phone; he didn't even have a lock on it. After pulling up his internet, I typed in my name and handed it back to him. I sat and watched as he read article after article about me. He even watched a few videos of my matches throughout the year. Every so often, he'd raise his eyes to look at me, give a small nod, and then his eyes would return to his screen.

"See, I don't hustle little kids for their lunch money, but if I had thought about that when I was younger, I'm pretty sure I would have."

"Of course, you would have. So, what did you like to do for fun as a kid if you were into chess?" Sitting his phone down I couldn't help but notice he was now on my social media page, personal not professional.

"Honestly? Nothing, when I wasn't training, I was still playing. If it wasn't in the park with the old heads, I was going against my father, who refused just to let me win because I was a kid. When they thought I got enough of that and no one would play against me I sat in the park and watched kids play. As I got older, I didn't have too many friends, so it wasn't like I was catching up on my sleep or hanging with my girls in my teenage years. Now I'm just settling into a routine which is going to change once the school years start, and I'm teaching."

"Plus, you'll be doing something else too." He said as he looked up from his food to make sure I was paying attention to what he was about to tell me.

"Oh yeah, what's that?" Finally, taking a bite of my food, I watched as he leaned forward, almost in a cocky manner, as if whatever he was about to tell me was going to be the best gossip ever.

"You'll be spending time with me too." His lopsided grin back in place and all I could do was smile as well. He didn't think twice about what he said, and he knew I wouldn't turn him down.

"What makes you think I'll be spending my time with you?"

"Easy, before we leave here, I'm going to ask you for

your number, you'll give it to me and then I'm going to call or text you tonight. I will ask you out on a date. We'll have fun on that date, getting to know each other and end it with the dopest good night kiss you will ever experience. We will repeat that action over and over. I mean, I doubt you're going to say no since our first date has gone so well."

"First date?"

"Yeah this is our first date.It's a two-parter actually." Taking a sip of his water, he looked so sure of himself. His confidence is sexy as hell. "Our first part of the date was the entertainment with that show from your neighbors, and now we are enjoying our meal. So, tell me what made you want to be a teacher?"

"I have my master's in education, and I didn't want it to go to waste."

'Really?"

"Yeah, really, why do you seem so shocked?"

"I'm not shocked; I'm impressed." He said, then licked his lips slowly. This man oozed sex appeal.

*<u>**Chance**</u>

"Nigga I'm not going to argue with you about this. I'm staying out of it, you fucked up, not me. You're the dumb ass that listened to Channing ole bitter ass." Drying my hands with a paper towel, I watched as my grown-ass brother sulked around my house as he tried to explain to me for the millionth time how Anlee wasn't talking to him. I didn't care and had other things on my mind. It has been almost a week since Queen and I had gone on our first date. Well, I told her that was considered a date. I planned to pull out all the stops when I got a chance to take her out again. If I wasn't talking to her. I was at the shop, we hired a few new artists, and two more had come down from our other locations to help out and get the flow going. When I wasn't busy with that. I sat in the back room and painted. And as bad as it sounds lately the only thing I could paint was Queen. I had not told her, but I planned to gift her a small painting I did of her. I just didn't know how to give it to her without looking like a creep.

"So, you not gonna help me out with this?" He looked surprised, like what I had been saying the last thirty minutes hadn't registered in his brain. He wore that same stupid ass expression on his face that Channing had a few days ago. I looked at him for a minute and walked off. I don't care what either one of my parents said they had to be doing drugs when my mama was pregnant with them and afterward because they were both slow as shit.

"No nigga now get out!I have a date to get ready for."

"With who?" He yelled from the living room; I could hear him booting up the game. If he thought, he was about to lounge around on my shit all day; he had another thing coming. "Yo, raggedy-ass easel and paints?"

"Not yo fuckin' business. Be out my shit by the time I get out the shower." I headed into the bathroom. If he wasn't gone by the time, I got out; I was calling my mama. She could deal with this slow ass nigga and his emotions. His cry baby ass always had jokes about me painting yet had at least five of them hanging in his house and three in his office. Silly ass nigga dropped the full price for them too because he couldn't keep his mouth shut.

"WHAT HAS YOU THINKING SO HARD?" Jess's voice caught me off guard, so I jumped a little. I was so wrapped up in my thoughts. I hadn't heard her come in. Looking over, I watched as she walked around, examining each painting, some she had seen before, and others she hadn't. Like the one of Queen sitting on a large 41"x40" canvas against the wall. I started it the day I hung out on her porch; it was of her standing in the door frame. Her dark skin shinning as the sun hit it, her hair pulled up high on her head, her locs so small that if you weren't paying attention, you would think her hair was just wavy. It was the small details that made you pause. Like how pouty her lips were, the slight pudge to her nose, her perfect oval-shaped face. Yeah, Queen is beautiful, and my painting did her no justice.

"Never mind, I see now." Smirking Jess stepped back from the painting, her eyes never leaving it. "I can't find an imperfection about her. Like I need her to have something wrong, a lazy eye, a lisp, be bow-legged, something you know?" She was a photographer in her spare time, she saw the beauty in everything, everyone but she also saw the bad. She liked the beauty but loved the bad.She once told me she enjoyed flawed people because they were easier to understand, I personally didn't think so but whatever.

"She's so stubborn, but she's gorgeous and funny, smart, can hold a conversation. You know how I am Jess; I get bored easily but with her.It's like we don't even have to talk, her being there is enough, and we haven't hung out a lot. We hung out like two times, and she's got me hooked."

"That's not a flaw." Laughing, Jess finally moved away from the painting and made her way over to where she kept her cameras. Those were her babies. She loved them almost, if not more than she loved Channing. She has been collecting them for almost her entire life. Her uncle gave her the first one when she was five. At the time, her mom had been admitted to the psych ward for the tenth time in her short life.

"What if I want more than sex too? Like a relationship" Leaning against the wall I watched as she took pictures of my paintings, they would be put on social media later.

"She wants sex, if we were animals that could smell pheromones, we would smell you two from miles away. The way yall look at each other. Boy, that shit is pure unreleased sexual tension. And there isn't anything wrong with sex, but intimacy is an amazing thing its far more delicate than sex. More special, but learn her first. It's so much better when you learn everything you can trust me on this one. I mean come on Chance I've been with Channing almost half my life. If you're anything like him in the bedroom, which I believe you are because I can't even start to count how many friends I've had to let go because of you, then the woman needs that experience. But and this is a big but if she doesn't want it then let it go. From what I've learned about her over the last month or two is she is extremely private, does her job, and then goes home. Doesn't bother anyone and is enjoying the possibility of a new career."She said as she clicked away at her camera. Jess was a multi-tasker; she had to be. Between running the shops, her photography business, and her sisters' pottery business she was a partner in as well. She was always doing something, helping someone, or watching over everyone. If she said stop and learn, then I had to listen. Even if I didn't want to but she had to tell me that first, that's the only way I would let the idea of Queen and I go.

"Wait a minute when did you see us together? We've only hung out once."

"At the bar about a week ago around lunchtime. I was meeting with Anlee about final payments for her work. We saw yall; even she said yall look good together." Turning towards me, she begins to walks backward so that she could still talk to me before she made her exit. "And Chance don't fuck this one up. I like her, and I like it here. It makes me want to put down roots." She said right before she disappeared around the corner.

NINE
QUEEN

"Even if you live in a small town, you're supposed to watch your surroundings still." Kin stood in front of me as I laid in my hammock, her workout clothes drenched with sweat. I had a bad habit of spacing out when I was out here; it was peaceful. I smiled up at her and waved her over.

"What are you looking at?" Walking over she made her way around to stand over my shoulder. She watched as I moved from one picture to another, each one more beautiful as the last. I found myself on Chance's social media page being nosey. He was a lot more talented than I expected. The social media page was filled with the most beautiful paintings I had ever seen. Black and white, watercolors, people, animals, places. You name it, and it was there. Thousands of pieces of amazing artwork done by someone I had met but downplayed his talent by saying he was just a tattoo artist.

"Yo who's page is this? These are amazing." I shrugged my shoulders without looking up at her.I pointed to the page name and waited for her to connect the dots. When she did her smile was bigger than it should have been.

“He has a couple of paintings I want to buy. Would it be rude if I just popped up at the shop or should I just send him a dm about it?”

"I'm going to shower.I still have a bag upstairs; then, we're going to their shop." She didn't wait for me to respond. There was no need, I was going to get that painting, because I wanted it. Even if I had to deal with Chance to get it. Even if he made me nervous, but I told Parker I would live outside the box and do what she would do., And knowing her, she’d pop up at his shop and demand not only his painting but for him to fuck me senseless. But since I wasn’t that crazy, I would only do one of those things.

The car ride over to the tattoo shop didn't take long; no ride around the city took long, 20 minutes top. Leaning against the seat, I watched Kin out the corner of my eye; she looked stressed but not as much as before.

"What's going on with you? I know you've been in your cave writing, but you still look stressed out."I said as we made our way down the street.

Sighing she looked over at me while we sat a stop light. "So, I've decided to change the genres." We made our way though town in no rush.We waved at people we knew and enjoyed the beautiful day.

"And?" Kin didn’t give you writer vibes, especially romance writer vibes, but it’s what she did besides run the bar. When she first told us about it when we met a few years back, I could honestly say I was surprised by it. But as I got to know her and we became friends. I was more surprised by the fact that she owned a bar. She was a romantic by heart, it was just her looks that didn’t say it.

"I'm about 30 thousand words into this story and I love it."

"Again, and?"

"It's a crime, I'm writing about a serial killer splash ex-spy." Pulling in front of the tattoo shop, I waited for her to get to the real reason she looked so upset. Okay, so she changed genre's writers did it all the time; It was okay to mix it up. Then it dawned on me, change she hated change.

"You're nervous that your romance readers won't follow you over to a new market?" It all made sense once she looked at me again, readers were picky sometimes, but Kin's readers were loyal.They preordered books weeks before they came out. They stood in lines to meet her at releases and when she had online chats; they flocked by the thousands to ask her questions. She was worried about nothing.

"Yes, Queen, you know how fans are, they want you to stick to what they know. Don't change. Nothing different. They want their book bae's, ride or die best friend, funny sidekicks, a little sex, a lot of fucking because there was a difference, a happily ever after and repeat." Rubbing her hands down her face I watched as she let her frustration go just for a little, Kin didn't need to stress there was no reason to.

"Kin, your fans will love whatever your writing about and if they don't, then that their loss. But hun, you have to let that fear go and do what your heart is telling you to do. If that means writing about an amazing serial killer slash spy.Then write the fuck out of that story and make them remember why they've been fans of yours for so long."

"And if they hate it?"

"Then keep moving, you are too talented to let this fear stop you from putting out what technically isn't even yours anymore."

"Okay, Jill Scott, I hear you." Laughing, we got out the car; she knew I was right. Well, actually, Jill Scott was right since I quoted what she said during her Verzuz battle with

Erykah Badu. As soon as I heard it, I thought of Kin and how she was with her writing. It was probably why she was so successful.She never kept her stories locked away in her head or computer. She gave the world everything, and in return, they loved her for it.

I have never been inside a tattoo shop. I didn't see the need, especially since I didn't care for needles. But this wasn't what I was expecting. All the tv shows made them look dingy and looked like they smelled like day-old cheese or something. The glossy bamboo floors, dark leather furniture, bright light from the sun beaming through the glass wall made it feel welcoming. Not welcoming enough to allow someone to burn ink into my skin but welcoming enough. But it was the big ass ocean mural behind the check-in desk that did for me. It looked so real.

"It smells like cherries in here." I said after taking a few sniffs of the air.

"What exactly is it supposed to smell like?" Kin said as she rolled her eyes and smirked at me. Her attention went right back to the folder I assumed had pictures of tattoo's.

"Not cherries." Shrugging, I peeked over her shoulder to see what she was looking at.Dragons, of course, it was dragons. She had a weird fascination with them, and had for as long as I could remember. "Don't add another dragon; your entire arm is already full of them."

"It's called a sleeve; I have a sleeve."

"It's called a lot of pain that you're stuck with when normal people just buy pictures of things they liked and hung them on their wall."

"I'm pretty sure that today's standards of normal can't be justified by you, Chess Queen."

Laughing, I couldn't help but admit she was right; I knew almost nothing about today's standards of normal. I lived in my little world of Chess and didn't apologize for it either. I'd enjoyed the little bubble I'd been living in until I hadn't. Now I watched TV like it was going out of style. I went from barely turning on the tv to binge watching everything that kept my attention on Amazon Prime and Netflix. It was bad at times that I had to turn on the sleep timer so the TV would shut off and I wouldn't be sitting on the couch all day.

"Now, what do we owe the pleasure of having you two in today?" Jess said. Crazy funny Jess, she was already smirking, eyes already laughing as she came to sit down next to Kin. "Are we getting a tattoo or a piercing? I personally always recommend either nipples or clit because during sex, they heighten the experience."

"The picture of Queen, the painting, she wants to buy it." Kin didn't even look up from the book; now she was on tigers I figured she was about to start another sleeve. "We saw it online, she wants it."

"You'll have to talk to Chance about it, he's the painter. I just post them and allow social media to do my job for me." Heading in the direction she pointed. I slowly shook my head, of course, I would have to talk to him. I couldn't just buy it from her and go on about my life.Nope, I had to see him, talk to him, deal with him. I'd been putting off seeing him as much as I could because this man's entire vibe did something to my body, I wasn't ready to explore.

TEN
CHANCE

"It's bigger than I expected. I thought it was small, like a 10x7 or something, not the size of an entire wall." Her voice, it was smooth, soft, yet held an edge to it that made you pause each time. I wasn't the nigga you read about in romance novels that knew from the moment he saw the chick he would fall in love with her and marry her, but I wasn't the nigga that played dumb either. Everything I said to Jess earlier was the truth. She stood in the door frame, today she wore some black high waist ripped jeans, with a fitted white tee that hugged her breast perfectly and chucks on her feet. Her locs were pulled high on top of her head, making her neck look good enough to lick.

" How did you see it?" I know Jessica posted it a little over an hour ago, but I doubt Queen followed any of us on social media. Any time we talked, she never mentioned her social media or the crazy number of followers she had. And she hardly posted on her personal page at all. And I should know, since she showed me her page, I basically stayed on that damn thing watching to see what she posted. Usually, it was just pictures of food, throwbacks of different times in her life. A few times, she posted a selfie or two, but that was it.

"How much?"

"A date." I leaned against the wall to watch her. She didn't step into the room; just watched me watch her. She didn't fidget; her eyes went from me to the painting and back, she was studying it. Her slight head tilts made it obvious e but only if you were paying attention and I was. The shock on her face was funny. She wasn't expecting me to mention going out again since I never brought it up while we were on the phone.

"A date?"

"Yep, well, no, not just one, four go on four dates with me and the paintings yours." I had no idea why I said four dates, all I know is I want to spend as much time with Queen as I could. She intrigued me, and my mom always told me growing up I was too nosey for my own good. That whole curiosity killed the cat thing, I guess. "Can you agree to that?" I asked.

"I could pay you for it," she responded.

"Or you could go on four dates with me, enjoy yourself and then get the painting. I think my offer sounds far, don't you?"

"But you don't even know which one I want." She said, and I couldn't even argue with her. I had some on there that I was asking a nice amount for. But that didn't matter.I could always paint something else; there was no telling when I would get the chance to ask her out again.

"Doesn't matter." Shrugging my shoulders, I said.

She stood there, just staring at me like she was going over her options in her head. Her entire face empty of all emotions, but it was her eyes, those beautiful grey and blue combination that let me know she was interested. Slowly she licked her lips and nodded her head then walked out the room. Maybe Jess was right our sexual chemistry was there and obvious. Now all I had to do is learn her mentally, which was the point of the dates.

"SON, I can't tell your brother what he already knows." My mother said as she chopped up whatever she was cooking for her and my pops dinner. I was tired of this nigga and he'd only been here for a few weeks, but it felt like years. Every damn day he sat around Anlee's office or house to talking to her. At one point, she called the police and had him arrested. And you better fucking believe I left his ass in jail for the entire weekend trying to teach him a lesson. Did it work? Hell no, it didn't! His stupid ass was right back in front of her house the next day.

"Ma! Your child is trippin, though! She's going to press charges if he doesn't leave her alone." I said as I laid out my clothes, preparing for my date later that day. It had been two days since Queen agreed to let me take her out on a date. I was in the middle of getting ready when my mom called.

"She's not going to press charges, Channing." She rolled her eyes at me and set down her knife to give me her full attention. Her dark brown skin glowed from the sun. My sister Charity, in the background, smiling brightly.

"And how do you know that?" Working quickly, I searched through my dresser drawer for the socks I wanted to wear.

"Because I talked to her. Well, we talk every week have since she left." I stopped what I was doing to look at her. Without thinking, I sat down on the bed and picked up the phone. She knew how lost Choice had been over the years, saw how guilty Channing acted after everything happen. But here she was sitting here talking to me. Telling me she and Anlee spoke weekly as if it was no big deal. "Close your mouth, son; you'll let a fly in if you don't."

"Charlene Douglass, you are sitting here telling me that you've been talking to your son's ex wife every week like he has not been showing his ass the entire time?"

"Watch your mouth, and I'm only telling you this so you can stop stressing and tell me about this girl you like so much."

"How do you know about Queen?"

"Son, I'm your mother. I know what you and your crazy ass siblings are doing even when you don't want me to."

"In other words that clown behind you still dancing told you everything?" Nodding to my sister, that was, in fact, still behind her dancing to only the beat in her head. My mom slightly laughed. Charity couldn't hold water to save her life. We knew not to tell her anything, but we ended up doing it anyway because she gave the best advice.

"Yes, now tell me about this Queen."

"How you know about Queen?" I asked.

"Didn't we already discuss the part about me knowing what yall doing when yall do it?" She said as she waved my sister out of her direction and away from her. Their dynamic was one that always made me smile. Growing up, they bumped heads because they were female, and it was bound to happen. But it was after Charity went off to college that the situation changed. She called home one night and asked her to come visit, and she had. From that point on, they were inseparable. Whatever happened on that trip changed them in the best way possible.

"Ma , she's so dope! She was a chess champion, a Grand

Champion or whatever it's called. And she is beautiful, funny, and smart as hell." Smiling, I listed the first few things that came into my head.

"So, tell me how you're going to go about this one differently." She started back up , chopping from what I could now tell it was celery. She knew my history with some. She knew how I never wanted anything from them but sex. I didn't hide it either; it was a mutual decision between two consenting adults. My mother, of course, hated it, but she respected the fact I didn't play with women's hearts. She always said when I knew who I wanted, I wouldn't hesitate to let it be known.

"I'm going to learn her, ma." When I said that, she stopped, looked at me for a second, and nodded her head. She knew exactly what I meant, and silently, she approved.

ELEVEN
QUEEN

I was on a date, one date out of four with Chance just for a picture he painted.I wasn't sure If I was nervous, happy, or excited. I wasn't a dating person; I mean, don't get me wrong I've been on dates before, but usually, it was something one of my girls set up. Usually with guys they knew wouldn't be used for anything besides a quick meal and possible sex and that was only if they didn't get on my nerves too quick. Which is more than likely the reason I had a standing dick order with Dr. Doctor.

"When did you do the painting?"

"The day after our first date." He looked good. Like damn good in his checkered red dress shirt, blue slacks, and red tie. Only he could wear suspenders with it and not look tacky. Again, his cut was perfect, I usually didn't like men with beards.I was over the whole #beardgang thing, but with him, it worked. It wasn't over the top long and bushy.It was tapered and lined up so well that it made his lips pop. The man was gorgeous, and he knew it. He wore it like a badge of honor.

"Why?" I wanted him to give this long explanation on

how he painted everyone, but I knew as soon as that thought popped into my mind, it was a lie. While I was getting ready earlier, Kin sat around, giving her unwanted opinion on everything I picked out to wear.

"I paint, draw, tattoo whatever you want to call it, and it's what I do. I see a picture in my mind whether it be a person, animal, location whatever it is, and I put it on a canvas, and it leaves my mind." He spoke with so much passion that it made me pause.The few times I'd seen Chance, he was always joking, always had a smile on his face. When we spoke on the phone, he was always asking questions, making sexual comments, or giving me some random facts about a place he had traveled or wanted to go to. This time he was serious. He had passion in his eyes; he was for lack of better words beautifully impassioned with the thought of art. In a way that I was passionate about Chess.

"How long have you been into art, and please don't say you're not because I saw your work. You downplayed it the other day while eating, but now I know better." The question made him pause.

"I'm not into art. I just like to draw." He shrugged, trying to play off his passion as if it made him look weak. When in all actuality it didn't. It made him look more handsome, more like a man being a man and not a boy pretending to be one.

"Who's your favorite?" I ignored him on purpose; he was into art. He was an artist, even if he didn't see it. His work spoke for itself.

"I don't have one, well, not anyone I could call my favorite. I have pieces that I love, the artist who I enjoy." He seemed deep in thought like I wasn't in the room, and he was picturing all the ones he enjoyed and others he didn't.

But it was his, whatever he was thinking about was his thoughts and his alone." No, none of them are my favorite."

"Frank Morrison, his Urban Jazz collection, that's who I thought you were going to say, or maybe Lois Mailou Jones. You seem to like that era is what you would enjoy." The shock on his face was comical at best. I didn't look like the type that knew anything about art. Honestly, I didn't, I only knew about those people because of my grandparents. They would sit around and talk for hours about people, their work, who if anyone was worth a damn these days. I bet they would all agree that Chance's work was worth a damn.

"Did you google those names before you came?" He laughed, the deep sound seemed like it came from the bottom of his gut. " If not impressed, I mean, we never talked about art before."

"No, but there are only a few that I know of. My grandparents love art, especially black art. They made sure to submerge us in it as much as possible. So, I know a little bit, nothing compared to them or even my cousin Jules. I know enough to hold a decent conversation for about it though."

He just stared at me for a while, I could see the smirk that he was trying to hide, and I couldn't help but want to laugh too. I paused, looked at my watch to check the time, and smiled as I looked back up at him. "Twenty minutes before the person realizes I'm full of shit and have no idea what I'm talking about, that's how long I can keep them going. But with you, it was only a few seconds." Again, he laughed, this time louder, deeper. The sound moved across my skin like a light breeze, and I loved it.

"You were pretty convincing, if you hadn't started to smile, I might have believed you. You don't look like you give a damn about art like that."

"So, I need to work on my poker face. I'll remember

that." Nodding my head, I let out a small laugh.He was right. I didn't give a damn about it. I just showed interest because it was easier growing up if I did. The most I cared about was how I did or didn't like or want to hang in my house.

"Nah, don't do that. I like being able to read you so well."

"Nope, can't have that at all." I wanted to offer to have my grandparents or parents look at his work, but for some reason, I didn't think he would like that. He seemed like he wasn't into handouts and took pride in earing everything he did. The thought popped into my mind before I realized it. He was good.There was no reason why they wouldn't like his work.

"You could try but I'm observant as hell and you are definitely worth studying." He said before he took a small sip of his drink, he ordered straight Hennessey. I watched him gulp the first down earlier, he wasn't drunk not even tipsy yet, but he was starting to get a buzz. I could tell from the glossy look in his eyes that wasn't there before.

"Okay, so what do you know about? If art isn't your specialty, then what is? Do you cook, speak five different languages? How many siblings do you have? You have talked about your grandparents, but what about your parents? What's the secret about the woman named Queen? Every time we text or talk on the phone, we talk about everything but ourselves." He leaned forward, placing his elbows on the table and face in his palms. Chance looked interested. Like whatever came out of my mouth would be the best thing he ever heard. Like my words carried the key to unlock the best-kept secret ever on earth. It was cute; this wasn't the crude crass Chance I met before, this guy was amazing, funny, and smart. This version of him could be the guy who added the change to my life.

"There's nothing special about me. I'm just a girl living in a small town that just started her new career as a teacher." The look that he gave me told me he didn't believe me. It was true I wasn't special.I was just a woman learning herself after spending countless hours pleasing the world with my talents." To answer your questions, yes, I can cook but only simple foods. I only speak English and some French. One sibling would have been enough, but my parents thought otherwise, so I have a few. My parents are alive and work as Curators and buyers for my grandparent's Art Gallery's." Looking around, I watched as the restaurant buzzed with energy, people laughing, others looked bored with their company. We went back to eating.Neither of us finding the words to say yet we were comfortable in our silence. We didn't need to rush words.

"Fine, I'm just going to ask you random questions all the time until I figure you out."

"I keep trying to tell you I'm boring, but go right ahead and ask away."

"Okay, question one, how did all yall become, friends? I mean, it's a dope mix up. The Cop, Therapist, Interior Designer, Bar Owner, and Chess Champion. Yall are five successful black women in a world that like to exploit yall in the negative spotlight. How do you all do it?"

"You know you could've started off with a simpler question.Like what's your favorite color?or what's your zodiac sign? Even, what do you like watching on Netflix? Do you like animals? You know stuff like that." I said laughing; if we were keeping score, he'd get the point for each career he remembered.

"Fine." He said, smiling as he thought over his question. "What's your favorite food to eat?"

I leaned back in my chair and smiled again. He purposely ignored the list of questions I have given him and asked what he wanted to know. Granted, it wasn't a hard-hitting question, so it was one I had no problem answering.

"Ice cream. It doesn't matter the flavor, but I do have a preference of going down to the ice cream store and having them mix me up something different each time I go. When I was a kid, I didn't eat it often, the thought of flavored milk didn't sound too appealing, so I always passed on the chance to have some. Little did I know I was missing out on something so amazing."

"So, you're making up for lost time?" He said as he cut into his steak. He was a meat-eater. I noticed the first time we went out; he ordered steak as well. Just like the first time, he sat in front of me and devoured it and didn't judge when I did the same with mine.

"Yep, I have a list of things that I didn't do as a kid that I plan on doing now."

"Like what?" He said in between bites.

"Nope, I can't tell you that easily. You are going to have to work to get that kind of information." I said. His smile bloomed across his entire face, the challenge I'd given wasn't necessarily hard. I had maybe twenty things that I wanted to do. I only told him to see if he was interested in getting to know me or getting me in bed.

"Bet," He said nodding his head in agreement

Music played softly in the background as Chance drove back to my house. Each song a different genre, yet they all seemed to flow together perfectly. Biggie, to Busta, to Missy to round it out with some Beyoncé. Each one he knew word for word. I couldn't help but to laugh. He was, without a doubt, the most complicated yet simple man I had ever met. The rest of our dinner showed just that. We eventually eased back into our conversation, but this time, I took the lead on the questioning. I asked about his family, and he told me about growing up in NY. His favorite thing to do was the sit on the block and listen to music. He ate pizza like it was going out of style, yet he hated the subway. He said it was too crowded and smelled like pee. We talked about his life. How he went to school for art history but was bored around his second year, so he dropped out and got an apprenticeship with a local tattoo artist. When he was done, he wanted to venture out on his own, so he talked his brother into helping him open a shop.

I didn't believe him though. There was no way this man, this amazing, could dismiss what he'd done with his life all by the age of thirty-three. I wasn't believing it. He may have thought he had me fooled, but he didn't.

TWELVE
CHANCE

Date two was nothing like our first date. She was more open and relaxed to the thought of us hanging out. Plus, I could tell she was having fun. Who wouldn't at an indoor bounce house. I thought she was going to tell me no when I first suggested it. I just knew she would, but when she said okay, my heart stopped for a second. Since she wouldn't tell me what was on her list, I thought back to things I had done as a kid with my friends and siblings. Every chance we got, we begged our parents to take us to the local bounce house so we could let loose. As a kid I didn't realize how much of a favor that was to our parents because after we were finished, we were too tired to do anything else but sleep. So, it was obvious why they jumped up every time we asked. Four kids in a three-bedroom apartment in New York was cramped as hell, so if we were going to be quiet even for only a few hours, they weren't going to complain. And as a bonus for me now, I could check out Queen's body without looking like a perv. I wanted to see her jump up and down, watch her ass and titties jiggle as she enjoyed herself. Yes, I'm aware I'm a pig, but hey, I was okay with it.

"They are starting the first round of dodge ball here shortly." Standing next to me, she read the board with all the times on it, dodge ball, it was her idea, said it would be fun. Personally, I didn't believe her, but who was I to tell her no? "After that, I want to do some laser tag, you down?" She wore those stupid contacts again. When she opened her front door when I got to her house, I tried to hide my disappointment. I like how she looks in her glasses more than the dumb contacts. We spoke that morning on the phone, and I told her to dress down, and she had, wearing a white and black Ivy Park swear suit with some white Adidas tennis shoes. I remember when the orange and maroon one dropped, and all the celebrities were posting when they got their boxes. I liked that one but seeing this one on her made me like it more.

I lost three games of dodge ball, two games of laser tag all to Queen. She ate this shit up, loved it honestly but was the best type of winner. She didn't celebrate, wasn't loud, just took her small trophy, smiled, and walked away.

"Since you won, I'll let you pick dinner." Holding the door open for her to get inside, Queen smirked rolled her eyes and got into the car. "I won because I'm better than you are." Yeah, so much for the humble and gracious winner.

"We can go somewhere simple. I'm just in the mood for a slice of pizza from The Quake and a bottle of orange juice if that's okay with you?"

"Pizza I'm down for, the orange juice part? Yeah, not so much. That don't even go together." I said as we got ready to move into traffic I watched as she got comfortable in her seat. The relax Queen was back. I'd learned there were many sides to her. She could be flirty, serious, fun, and relaxed. I like relaxed Queen the most. She smiled, laughed like no one was listening, and danced like no one was watching, and if they were, she didn't care. "So why orange juice?" I had to know. It didn't make sense to me; I was from NY, we ate pizza and drank beer, ate hot dogs, and drank beer. Basically, we ate and drank beer with everything.

"When I was a kid and on the road every morning when my grandparents would be getting ready for the day. They would sit down and have a cup of coffee. I asked to taste it because I, like any kid, was nosey. Let's just say I threw up over the entire hotel room, like the whole thing, curtains, beds, floor, walls, and if you let my grandma tell it, I even hit the ceiling. The only thing after that I wanted was orange juice.I hate coffee with a passion if I even see coffee, let alone smell it for long periods; it makes me nauseous. So orange juice became my thing. I drink it all the time. No matter what time it is or what I'm eating. I've become addicted to it in a sense. My day isn't complete if I haven't had a jug or two. " Laughing, she rolled her eyes at me and turned towards the window. I made a mental note for later. Queen liked orange juice, and hated coffee. I also noticed she always had something on orange. Take now, for instance, She wore an orange tank top on to finish off her look. Another thing to note was it seemed like she was a shoe freak. Every time we talked, and I asked her about her outfit for the day, she mentioned a different pair of shoes. They weren't always heels either in fact, most of the time, she mentioned tennis shoes.

"SHE DOESN'T WANT me for shit. I mean not finically at least. She has her own, and I'm enjoying the whole getting to know you process." Taking a puff of my cigar, I watched how my brothers responded, yeah, they could front all they want, but I know the type of men they are. They could front for the world, but I know the truth. We'd decided to meet up at The Cigar Club which was ran by three brothers in town. Black men at that, the amount of black people around here surprised me. And to top it off, most of them were business owners or worked for black businesses. This place gave you small town vibes but progressive small-town vibes. Even the vibe here was laid back, not a lot of the younger crowd. Mostly business people or men, in general, enjoying themselves without the loud and over the top atmosphere. This was a professional man type of setting. We'd been discussing the kind of women we were attracted to when the hostess brought us over another drink and cigar.

"She not your normal style though.She not flashy, don't wear the long weave, have the long-ass nails. She not rocking the designer's none of that shit. I mean she is natural, but it works for her.I couldn't see her any other way." Choice said as he puffed away.The entire Anlee situation was weighing heavy on him. You could see it in the way he carried himself.He wasn't sloppy or anything, but he wasn't his regular put together confident self.

"That's the point, she ain't like them, yet she keeps my attention. When we are together it's like I'm kicking it when my finest friend, who I happen to want like no other." Checking my phone, I noticed the time. I had a tattoo to due in the morning that would take about eight hours, so I planned to wrap it up soon.

"So, you trying to lock her down?"

"Queen? Hell yeah, I'm locking her down."

Someone clearing their throat caught my brothers and I attention.Turning to the right, there stood a nerdy-looking dude in faded blue jeans, black polo, and black dress shoes.

He could only be around 5'10 and slim as hell but dude looked pissed. His chin us square in shape, he has a pointy nose, and beady eyes that sat behind some dumb ass looking glasses. His cheeks are flushed, and his ears are red. He looked like he was ready to let it all loose on me, yet I know for a fact I've never seen his ass before.

"Can we help you?" Channing said from my right, glancing over, I could tell he got the same vibe from him as I did. The thing is none of us felt threatened, and the only reason I know that is because we hadn't even gotten up from our seats.

"The woman you're speaking about is already spoken for." Point Dexter said as he crossed his arms over his chest as if that would intimate us or something. I mean dude was so skinny that the sleeves on his shirt around his biceps dangled around him.

"What, woman?" Standing up, he realized how much I towered over him, which caused him to step back a little. But I had to give it to him. He didn't let the fear show too much.

"Queen, she's already spoken for."

"By whom?" Channing asked from his seat. I heard Choice try to cover up his laugh and I cracked at smile at Channing. For a nigga who talked so much shit and clowned the majority of his life, he couldn't help but use proper English. As ignorant as he allowed people to perceive him as he could conquer anything that he put his mind to. Except how to stay out of other people's relationship. That shit seemed to fly right over his head like rocket science did majority of the world.

"Me, we've been dating for the last two years." Stepping back up, he looked as if he was ready to go all-in for Queen.

I mean I couldn't blame him, but the nigga was about to get his feelings hurt and embarrassed.

"My man, I can tell you right now ain't no way in hell you been dating Queen for no two years." Laughing slightly, I sat back down in my seat. This nigga wanted attention I wasn't giving him. My brothers nodded their heads in agreement and leaned back in their chairs.

"I most certainly am telling you that. So, I would advise you to stop speaking her name."

"And if he doesn't?" Choice said from his seat as he leaned forward with his elbows resting on the top of his thighs. He rubbed his hand over his beard as he waited for ole boy to respond. His actions were another sign he wasn't in his typical relaxed nature. Choice wasn't the short-tempered let's fight kind of dude at least night anymore.

"Then, we can step outside and handle this like men." Sizing us up without a second thought he walked away. I looked at my brothers, who shrugged their shoulders and laughed. Without looking down at the bill, Channing threw two hundred dollars down, and we headed towards the door. It seems like Queen had niggas fighting for her honor and didn't even know it.

"Did this nigga just challenge yo ass to a duel? Where the swords at? Nigga you about to be outside fencing, talking about on guard!" Channing said laughing.I told you the nigga was dumb as shit sometimes. Pushing past Channing, Choice and I made our way outside with him pulling up the rear, still trying to get control of his laughter.

When we made it out there, he stood with three other dorky looking dudes waiting for us. We weren't the let's talk this out kind of men. Especially when we were called out, it was the New York in us. If you wanted rowdy and loud, I could give you that, if you wished to be gentlemen I could give you that. If you wanted that gutter style nigga best believe you were going to get that. And it looks like ole boy wanted the gutter style nigga.

"Now gentlemen, what the fuck is going on here, Dr. Doctor, I know you aren't out there trying to show out, are you?" Turning, I watched as Parker, Anlee, and Queen made their way towards us. They were dressed down, jeans, t-shirts, and jackets since it had been raining all day.The air had a slight chill to it. I nodded my head to Queen, signaling for her to come over to me, which she did without a second thought. We embraced for a quick hug. I didn't completely let her go when she stepped to my side.I left my arm around her shoulders.

"You going to answer Parker's question?" She asked me softly as she leaned her head against me.

"Ask your boyfriend over there." I said, nodding my head towards Point Dexter, who looked about ready to pop his lid. I watched as Parker rolled her eyes, and Anlee tried to hide her amusement by faking interest in cars passing us.

"He is not, nor has he ever been my boyfriend." Queen said, looking over at him; her lack of interest in him was apparent. But you could tell it was some history there from his body language.

"Then what do you call it?"

Before she could answer we heard Parker and Anlee laughing behind us. I turned around to see what was so funny, and I could see even my brothers were trying not to laugh at them. Parker was leaning against the light post, trying to keep her balance as Anlee stood there laughing and trying to look innocent.

"What did she sign?" One of the nerdy dude's friends said. Smirking, she signed some more; if I wanted to translate, I wouldn't have been able to with how fast her hands were moving. Apparently, Queen, Parker, and Choice understood everything she was saying because I felt Queen trying to hold in her laugh.

"She said this isn't the type of conversation your friend wants to have in public and advised you all to leave it alone." Parker said as she tried to level out her breathing and get herself together. Something told me from the look on Anlee's face that isn't exactly what she said.

"Good thing we weren't talking to you bitch." Said one of Point Dexter's friend.He looked like he was the type of nigga that hit women because they intimated him. He was the type of nigga that my brothers and I never rolled with, and before I could catch him, Choice had swung on him. That was all it took before both Channing and I were beating the shit out of all four of them.

THIRTEEN
QUEEN

"You were not supposed to be fighting! I didn't ask you to fight for me!" I watched as Anlee snatched Choice's hand and examined it.Her anger visible as she checked it for injury. What exactly she was angry about, I'm not so sure of. "How many times, huh? We went through this how many fucking times?! I told you it's not worth the damn fight."

"He disrespected you! Called you out your name, and you expected me to stand there? To just be some type of bitch nigga and allow that? You know me better than that! You already know how we get down back home! That shit ain't where it's at." He slapped his chest with every question he asked. Towering over her short frame, she didn't back down, didn't even look afraid of him at all, and let me tell you he looked scary as shit. Out of all the brothers, he looked like he lived in the gym and ate little nigga for breakfast, lunch, and dinner.

"You were supposed to let me handle it! Me not you! I've dealt with shit my entire life.Well, before you made your presence known and well after you leave. I handle shit as I see fit! Not you! I don't want you coming in here and showing your ass because you see fit! I don't want this type of shit in my life. I don't need this!" Again, she didn't back down, she looked him straight in the eye and spoke her mind And even though I didn't want to.I understood everything she was feeling. She made a life here without him.She lived the last eight years living the way she saw fit, and he had no right to come and try and change it. I watched as it was apart of him that looked as if he was ready to hit the wall because of his anger.Another part of him looked defeated. I knew pieces to their story, and I knew Anlee, some of what she said was true.She didn't need him to fight her battles. The part about not wanting him? That I knew was a lie.

I watched as my friend walked away from him, right out the door, and didn't look back, and surprisingly, Choice ran right behind her. Parker and Channing had only dropped us off, so that left just us at my house. But before she left Parker reminded me about the conversation, we had about tried something new and just going with the flow. She not so discreetly pointed at Chance and told me to fuck him as if my life depended on it. I pushed her out the door while she laughed the entire time.

"So, you want to talk about what was going on before we walked up?" I said as I got comfortable on the couch. I pulled the black throw I had on the back of the couch over me and adjusted one of the pillows under my head.

"Dr. Nerdy was trying to defend your honor by claiming you when he overheard my brothers and me talking about you." He said as he adjusted himself to get more comfortable on the other end of the same couch I was sitting on. He wasn't banged up; his knuckles were little raw from striking them, but that was it. He had blood splatter on his shirt and shorts and even his shoes, but you couldn't tell anything had happened less than an hour ago.

"His name is Joshua Marshall, Dr. Joshua Marshall and we messed around for a few years. Nothing more or less than that. We weren't in a relationship." I said laughing at the name he called Joshua, I knew he heard Parker call him Dr. Doctor earlier.Why they chose to change his name was beyond me.

"Just a hookup, huh?"

"Yep, we had fun for a while. Obviously, he was more invested than I was. This is exactly what the girls told me, but I didn't believe them." Shrugging, I got up and made my way to the kitchen. I wasn't remotely interested in Joshua on more than a sexual level. We had that conversation before we first started messing around. I explained to him from the beginning that a relationship and my schedule wasn't a good idea. The conversation I had with the girls not too long ago about him not being for me played in the back of my mind.

"I haven't seen him since I retired, we haven't even spoken, so I'm not sure where our wires got crossed." I damn near jumped out of my skin when I turned around, and he was standing behind me.

"So, you aren't interested in him?" He said as he softly gripped my neck, forcing me to look at him again. His dark eyes and deep timber of his voice damn near had my knee's about to give out. With his other hand, he softly ran his thumb across my bottom lip. Without thinking I slowly opened my mouth and bit down gently when he put it in my mouth and sucked on it gently. I heard the soft grunt he let out when I did.

The ringing of my phone broke the momentt.Looking over at the screen, I saw my grandparent's name as my screen glowed. When it stopped.I looked back over at him.I didn't want it to go too far just yet.

"I think you should go." I said just above a whisper to him. I couldn't speak louder than that without my voice giving away how much I wanted him. As I walked to the door, he didn't argue with me. Simply nodded his head and headed to the door. I watched him as he walked to his car, got in, and left. No, I wasn't remotely interested in Joshua, and if I were, I wouldn't have been by the time he left. We hadn't even done anything sexual, and my body craved his touch. His smell made my body ache and his voice? If I could get pregnant off his voice, then I'd be carrying multiples by now. So no, Joshua didn't stand a chance.

I called my grandparents back, and they were arguing.No, I take that back my grandparents didn't argue, they debated. They said their peace and went on about their lives. I can't remember a point in their entire relationship when they argued.They respected each other too much to argue. We were facetiming again; this time, grandma oversaw the phone, and things were going more smoothly. I hadn't seen their ceiling, floor, the fish tank, nor had the screen gone black because of grandpa pushing buttons.

"Queen, what do you mean you have someone's artwork you want to look into bringing into the new line up?" My grandmother looked as if she wanted to shake the shit out of me. I didn't always make the best decisions when it came to art. I didn't have an artistic bone in my body. I could only draw stick people and sometimes those didn't even turn out right. But I meant it when I said Chance was a fantastic painter. I knew once they saw some of his work, they would agree. Even though he said he wasn't interested in me putting in a word for him, I had anyway.

"Granny, he's good, I swear."

"That's what you said about that last boy and he was shit." Grandpa yelled from somewhere behind the screen, more than likely he was eating again. Grandma cooked earlier today day, and according to her, he was on his third bowl of greens and hot water cornbread, which was the only thing she could make that was decent.

Laughing, I couldn't help but shake my head. They would never let me live down the only other time I recommended someone." Grandpa I was seven and I thought his goldfish were amazing!" I had been trying to make friends; it was hard being one of the few black people and fewer black girls who played Chess on a competitive level at a young age. When a little mixed boy named Jason Long showed me his finger painting, I begged my grandparents to hang it in their gallery. After they sat me down and explained to me that his paintings were shit even at seven. I vowed to never tell them about any other boys art.

"You are partially blind. You have to be if you thought those damn things were great." Chuckling grandpa didn't care if I thought I was doing the right thing back then. Now I could laugh at it but then? Oh no then I was heartbroken. I didn't talk to either one of my grandparents for about two weeks. They did notcare, though.They said that tournament was the most peaceful because they didn't have to hear my mouth unless I was asking something or answering a question they asked. Mad or not I was no fool. Whenthey asked me questions, no matter how mad I thought I was, I answered. I knew they would whoop my ass if I thought I was going to be able to be disrespectful.

"Oh, Gabriel, leave the girl alone." Waving him off she turned back to me. "Queen what's that boys name, I'll look up his work on instaface or facegram." I didn't correct her. No matter how many times I told her the names correctly, she always said them wrong. Apart of me thinks she does it on purpose to annoy me, but who knows; maybe she didn't. After giving her his name. I watched as she worked the computer next to her. Her face went completely blank as she looked through his work. It was another thing I got from her. That resting bitch face that she had mastered well before it had become a thing. Sliding the laptop over to grandpa, she turned to look at me. I was nervous, I wasn't sure why but I was.

"Queen, is there anything you need to tell me about this young man?" She watched me, studied my face through the screen and waited. Did I mention I hated facetiming with my grandma? Not because I didn't enjoy talking to her because I loved it, but because she could see me. When I wanted to lie to her, I couldn't because she could see me. And everyone told me whenever I lied; I rubbed my ear lobe. If she could see me, then she would know when I was lying, like now, I wanted to lie but I couldn't.

"No ma'am." Looking everywhere but at her. I waited for her to call me out on my shit. Instead, she continued to wait. Just staring at me. Slowly blinking, her dark caramel skin glistening her grey and blue eyes sparkled as the sun hit her. Grandma didn't believe a word I said verbally or non.

"Bullshit!"

"Sunny, leave the girl alone! Queen, these are amazing!" Grandpa yelled again. He was back eating, but I could see him in the corner of the screen as he looked at the laptop and scraped his bowl for the last of his meal. "Tell him to call us."

Pressing the end button, he hung up without allowing me to say another word. She knew I was lying, well technically I wasn't lying there was nothing to tell. Chance and I have only been on two dates, but we did text every day for hours at a time. We hung out whenever we got the opportunity. If he wasn't painting or tattooing and I wasn't getting my lesson plans together, we were talking about anything that popped into our minds. We were just friends, and the more time I spent with him or talking to him made me realize I wanted more.

His social media page hadn't changed in the last few weeks; he added new painting and took down the ones he sold. There were a few of him and his brothers working out or just goofing around. He even had a few hoe shots mixed in there. His groupie fandom had no problem leaving heart eye emoji on them all. It was like he knew I was checking out his page because my phone rang in my hand, scaring me and making me double tap on a picture.

"Hello?" I said after putting in on speaker while I tried to get back into the app. I was on to, unlike the picture before he noticed.

"Hey gorgeous, you busy tomorrow? I know it's a school day, but I was hoping after you're done for the day, we could hang out for a little." He said as the background got quieter and quieter. He was more than likely on his way back to the shop. He texted me earlier in the day and told me he would be busy helping Jess with her photoshoot she had set up for the Cigar Club.

"Nope, in fact, tomorrow is a half-day so we can meet up early if you want."

"Cool, let's say we get together around two-thirty?" He said I could hear him typing away as we talked.

"That works for me." I finally found the picture I accidentally liked and unliked it, but not before taking one last look.

"Alright, hey, I have to go. I'll call you later. Is that okay?" He said I could hear him starting up his car.

"Yeah, I have to get ready for the girls to come by anyway." I said, getting up out my chair and pushing it into the island. I needed to straighten up a little before they arrived.

"Oh, and Queen." He said before I hung up.

"Yeah?"

"You didn't have to, unlike the picture." He laughed and hung up the phone. It would be my luck that he saw it before I could undo it. Setting my phone down on my coffee table, I yelled for Alexa to start my cleaning playlist.

"WHY DO YOU LOOK SO LOST?" Standing in the middle of the kitchen, Cooper looked as much out of place then I felt. She was not domestic, couldn't boil water without burning it. Kin stood near the stove cooking up meat for the Philly cheesesteaks she was making.

"He's drawing me." I flopped down in the bar stool chair that sat at the island in the kitchen. It had only taken me a about thirty minutes to clean up my kitchen, living room, and dining room, but once the music started getting good, I found myself cleaning the entire house. Just as I hopped out of the shower, I heard my phone ding. When I checked it, I had about thirty notifications from IG; Chance had tagged me another post. This time it was a picture of me sleeping. My head against a window, it looked to be a car because of the shape of it and the blurred background. He had titled it *Sweet dreams*. It already had over five thousand likes and hundreds of comments. Some good others jealous women and come men taking shots at anything they could find fault in. Instantly I liked it, set my phone down, and started getting ready for my night.

"Who?" Parker said as her red, blonde, and sandy brown hair all but forgotten about as she failed to pull it into a high ponytail.

"Chance, look." Sliding my phone towards her. I watched as they studied the pictures, there were at least ten more since I had been on earlier today. Some I knew from when we were together but others not so much. We'd only been out twice, even though we'd seen each other or talk all the time.

"Damn, these are amazing." She swiped, enlarged, and swiped again. She was right; they were each one of them.

"Kin, what the hell am I supposed to do?" Falling back in the chair, I threw my hands in the air. No one was helping, no one was telling me what to do about that crude, foul-mouthed, sexy, tall, giant that could paint me a thousand different ways and made my panties wet with just a simple smile or laugh.

"You said you wanted to change, and you wanted some adventure. Well, ma'am, you have found it in the name of Chance Douglass." Parker said laughing. She went back to work, trying to fix her ponytail. Usually, I would help her, but not this time. If I were struggling, then so would she. "That's what you get for wishing for something different."

Groaning, I dropped my head onto the island; what in the world did I get myself into? And how do I get out of it?

Wait.

Did I want to, though?

FOURTEEN
CHANCE

She looked innocent as hell as she sat on the park bench and ate her ice cream. We had agreed to meet up for lunch since school had let out early for the day, and she had nothing planned. I had a tattoo appointment later, but I wanted to spend time with her. When she looked up at me as I walked over, I couldn't help but smile back at her when she smiled at me.

"Am I late?" I asked as I sat down next to her on the bench. Sitting my backpack on the ground in between my legs.

"Nope, I didn't want any real food, just ice cream." She said in between licks.Her pink tongue swiping away at the orange-colored treat. I can't even lie; I was a little jealous.

"Good, finish up. I want to do something." Adjusting myself on the bench, I watched as she paused just slightly and looked at me. I watched as her eye traveled from my shoes all the way up to the top of my head. There were a few places she stopped and stared at for a second or two, but she didn't say anything.

We sat in silence for a while as she finished.Once she wiped her hands and face with a wet wipe, she kept in her purse; she turned her full attention on me.

"So, what are we doing?"

Smirking I pulled the two pair of skates out my bag.Handing her pair I watched as she sat them down on the bench between us.I waited as she looked at them then back at me. "You're supposed to put them on."

"I'm aware of that. I'm trying to figure out why." The skates were still on the bench, waiting for her as I started putting on mine.

"Remember when we were out not too long ago, and you said you didn't have much of a childhood because of chess?" I asked as I laced up the first shoe, still, she hadn't moved.

"I didn't say I didn't have a childhood; I said there were certain things I didn't do because I was busy playing chess." She said. Today she wore an orange Nike sweatsuit with black forces. Her hair was down, and it took everything in me not to touch her hair. My favorite thing was she didn't have on contacts. She had on those glasses I saw her in at the airport..

"Okay, answer these questions for me, and if you say yes to any of them, I'll beg and plead for your forgiveness and do anything you want me to do." I finished tying up my other skate and stood.

"Okay." She said as she turned her body straight so that she could look at me. She shielded her eyes from the sun as she tilted her head up.

"Can you ride a bike?" I asked as I slid forward a small amount.

"No."

"Ever popped fireworks?" Again, I moved up just a small amount.

"No, we grow up celebrating Juneteenth." I nodded my head at her answer.

"Double Dutch?"

"Not to save my life."

"Played stickball until the streetlights came on?" I moved up double the amount this time since I didn't move last time.

"No."

"So, guess what?" I asked. As I bent down into her personal space.Our breaths mixed as she inhaled, and I exhaled.

"Change your shoes, and get your ass up, you're learning to skate." I said and moved back laughing as Iswayed my body left to right, making sure I kept balanced so I wouldn't fall. The hardest part of this learning someone was understanding boundaries. As much as I know Queen wants me. I couldn't cross that line. At least night yet. I watched as she laughed slightly and did what I said, that was a lot easier than I thought.

"If I fall, I'm telling my daddy, and I'm pretty sure he'll shoot you." She said as she took off her shoes.

"It's easy," I said as I moved back and forth in front of her impatiently, waiting for her to finish.

"I DON'T GIVE two fucks what you say from here on out, that shit was not easy at all," Queen said as she grabbed plates from the kitchen cabinet. We'd been back at her house long enough to each shower, get into some comfortable clothes, order take out, and now we were relaxing in the living room.

"It is easy!You were just too scared to relax." I said laughing as I took the food out the bag. I doubled over in laughter when a paperwork roll came flying at my head.

"Obviously, I was supposed to be scared. Do you see all these scratches I have on me? How am I supposed to explain this to my students on Monday?" Making her way over to the couches, I watched as she seemed to glide over the floor, her steps barely making a sound.

"You are a bad listener, use it as an example for your students as active listening."

"No, what I'm going to do is tell them my new friend tried to kill me on some dangerous ass skates even though he was aware I didn't know how to skate." Sitting down next to me on the floor, she handed me my plate and silverware. We'd chosen Thai as our dinner tonight, usually, I wasn't big on Asian food, but Queen had invited me over to hang out after my client had called to reschedule her appointment for next week.

"Don't go lying to them kids about your nonexistent near-death experience to gain points in your favor." I handed her the egg rolls as I pulled out my fork.

"They will believe me too. One look at you and all your tattoo's, and they'll know you tried to kill me. Watch what I tell you." Nodding her head, she closed her eyes and said a quick prayer. Each time we've been out, she always did and would make sure I said mine too.

"Alright then bet, come here, let's take a picture so they can see what I look like. If you arectelling this story, I know you're going to make me into some giant monster with a thousand eyes and large head. These kids gotta know the truth." I pulled her into my legs, so her back was facing my front, she came without protest, and even though I could see the smirk on her face, I didn't call her out on it. Grabbing my phone off the table I pulled up the camera and took a few pictures. Some serious, other silly, but my favorite was of her smiling bright into the camera as I leaned my face into the side of her neck. Kissing it softly, I felt her exhale slowly, I wanted to do more and even planned on it, but the sudden ringing of my phone this time pulled me away.

"Looks like we were saved by the bell again, huh?" She said as she moved away.I watched her for a second before my phone stopped ringing only to start back up. It was a number I didn't recognize and almost sent it to voicemail, but I needed a breather away from Queen.

"Hello?" I said as I picked up the phone and stepped into the kitchen away from her. She had an open floor plan, the division of the kitchen and living room was an island that had the sink in it. Her small dining table set near the hallway that leads to the bedrooms and bathroom. Surprisingly, she didn't have any orange in her color scheme. The kitchen had dark blue upper and lower cabinets with stainless steel appliances. The counters looked granite, but I knew they weren't because when I complimented her on them when I first got here, she told me they were a poxy blend that cost a quarter of the cost of granite. It was impressive to look at.

"Yes, hello, may I speak to Chance Douglass, please." The voice on the other end said. I couldn't place them, but the loud, busy commotion in the background caught my attention.

"This is him." I said as I investigated her backyard from the patio door, she had slightly open to let the breeze come in. From all the loud ass sounds from the bugs outback, I'm glad her had her screen door closed.

"Hi, my name is Zeek Morrison I work for Brown Art Gallery. I am calling on behalf of the owners. They are interested in some of your pieces and wondered if you would like to meet with them?"

I looked over at Queen, who was now sitting on the couch on her phone.Whoever or whatever she was looking at had her full attention as she ate. Her long legs were hanging over the side of the couch, her plate sitting on the table across from her. I loved that she showed no fear of eating around me; she wasn't shy about too much. Especially about her body, she wore her skin with confidence and more sex appeal in her pinky finger than most women did in their entire body.

"Yes, of course, when would they like to meet?"

"Next weekend, if possible, they are having a youth art exhibit and would love for you to come into town and see it as well as talk to them in person. You could bring a guest and, of course, all expenses on us."

"Yes, I will be there. I'm guessing since you have my number, you have my email address too?"

"Yes, I have it. I look forward to meeting you in person next weekend. Have a good night." He hung up the phone and I just sat there. I'd heard of Brown Art Gallery had even been to a few of their shows, and they were interested in my work? Looking over I noticed Queen she was now into the movie we had picked to watch. It was like she felt me looking at her because she turned towards me with a big smile on her face.

"Everything okay?" Without looking up at me she continued to eat. Laughing, I watched as she did her food shimmy dance that all women did when they were excited about eating something.

"Yeah, you busy next weekend?" I questioned as I sat down next to her and grabbed my food. I can't even lie. I was nervous as hell about meeting with the Brown group, but I didn't want to mention it yet just in case it didn't work out. I didn't want to jinx it, it was still fresh, plus it was only a meeting.

"Yeah, why? You trying to kill me again with an easy adventure like rock climbing or deep-sea diving?"

"Nah, man, I was going to ask if you wanted to go somewhere with me next weekend." As down as I was with doing new stuff my black ass was not about to be rock climbing or deep-sea diving. Plus, Clarksville didn't even have mountains and we damn sure wasn't close to a fucking ocean.

"If I hadn't agreed to help Anlee, I would, maybe a rain check?" She said she seemed genuinely sad that she had to turn me down.

"Definitely a rain check."

For the rest of the night we watched movies, ate and talked, it was a little after three when I finally left.

"TEACH ME TO PLAY CHESS." I said as I watched her put away the dishes from last night. After a long day at the shop, all I wanted to do was chill out at home, but as soon as I got there, I realized I didn't want to do that either, so I called up Queen, who, of course, had no problem hanging out. The entire drive over, I realized I spent most of my free time with her, and when we weren't together, we were talking and texting all day. Our routine wasn't something I expected, but it was something I couldn't see myself letting go of anytime soon.

"You want me to do what?" Turning around to face me, she looked a little skeptical about the idea. Today she didn't have on anything orange, just some black biker shorts, grey shirt and of course some damn fuzzy socks.

"Since I took you out of your comfort zone with the skating, I want to do something you enjoy. Since Chess is your thing, then teach me." I went over to the entertainment center she had in her living room that houses almost every video game console I could think of; I pulled out the glass chess board she had on display.

"You really want to learn, or are you just doing this so that you won't have a guilty conscience." Wiping her hands on a napkin, she watched me as I made my way to the coffee table to sit down the board. I'd watched plenty of her matches on the internet. Each time I found myself stuck just watching how her confidence never wavered. Even as a child, she sat with her back straight, eyes focused on the board, and the move her opponent used against her. Each time she sat in her seat with the confidence of the queen that she was.

"Nah, like legit, I want to learn. You got a room full of trophies, awards, plaques, and pictures from you playing and it got me interested." Adjusting the pillow behind me I leaned back against the base of the couch and waited.

Nodding, she made her way over to me, taking a seat on the floor opposite me; she moved the board to the middle of the table. She picked up a piece that had what looked like a crown on it, she rolled it between her hands.

"Do you know the objective of the game?" She said without looking up at me, her eyes still stuck on the board and the different pieces.

"Yeah, to win."

"Yes, but do you know how?" She softly sat the piece back on the board when her eyes finally landed on me.

"Obviously not, which is why I want you to teach me." Pulling out my phone, I hit the playlist; I always listened to when I painted.

"Fine, first, let me tell you the pieces names and what they can or can't do. After that we will just start with some basics and go from there."

And she did just that; she cleared the entire board off and for each piece she sat back down, she explained what its role was. It took her about thirty minutes with me, stopping her every so often to go over something I wasn't sure about.

"So, the most important piece is the queen, then, right?" I said as I moved the pawn piece, this was our eighth game, each time she allowed me to get more and more moves in. The first few games she literally won in less than ten moves. She showed absolutely no remorse and would laugh at me when I tried to figure out what the hell had happened.

"Yes and no. The queen can move anyway and anywhere she wants, so she's the most dangerous, but she's expandable. If she's captured, it's a sacrifice that doesn't stop the game."

"But that's not said for the king though. If you lose him, then you lose the game." I said remembering what she told me when she broke down the rules.

"Right, but the king? He has limitations and once you capture him?"

"Game over," I said, watching as she moved her piece to sit directly in front of my king piece.

"Its called checkmate, but yeah, you get the point." She said, knocking over my king and smiling up at me. It was the same smile that she gave me in the kitchen when we first kiss. The cocky yet shy smile that made my dick hard as a rock. I had to bend my knee up to hide my shit; this girl was like playing with fire at times. Shaking my head, I picked the pieces back up and reset the board. It been a few months since I had sex, I hadn't fucked or anything since the night I had a threesome with Stevie and her friend.

FIFTEEN
QUEEN

"What do you mean the park wasn't considered a date?" I asked as I worked on my lesson plan. Chance sat beside me, going over his sketches. It has been a little under two weeks since we hung out at the park, and I could honestly say I missed him. Today he had on a pair of grey sweatpants, black tank top and some Nike slides, he officially had on the male version of thot attire, and he looked damn good. My orange sweatpants, white fitted t-shirt, and fuzzy socks matched his laid-back approach to the evening. We were both relaxed and comfortable.

He invited me over to hang out before our weekend got busy and our families came into town. Because his brothers were both mopping around his apartment with women problems, we opted to hang out at my house again, which I preferred anyway. We have been working for nearly three hours, only stopping to eat a quick meal, and we were right back at it.

"It wasn't a date; we were just hanging out after school. You know, like when you were a kid, and you spent time with your friends after school." He said without even looking up from his work. I sat back in my seat and watched as he worked, his concentration entirely on his work.

"Nope, I didn't do that as a kid, remember?" I said as I got back to my work. If I stared at him too long, I will end up saying something I shouldn't.

"Oh yeah, I forgot your childhood was dismal, and almost horrifying." He said, laughing.

"It was not dismal, you jerk. I had fun in my own way. I spent my free time when I had it watching my sister play basketball or being a test dummy for all my younger sisters meals. I'm not going to lie. She's probably the reason I love food so much now." I said as I got up to put my stuff away. I'd seen enough of little kids handwriting to last me for a few days. Plus, I had to get myself into a decent headspace to deal with my family.

"So, you're telling me I have one of your sisters to thank for what I'm seeing." He said I could hear him pushing his chair back from the table. As I put my laptop away, I never heard him get up, but I could feel his eyes on my body.

"And what exactly do you see?" I said, turning around so I could lean against the wall. I was right. He had leaned back in his chair, legs wide with is feet planted. The cocky smirk on his face all but disappeared as he licked his lips. His eyes so focused on my entire body I got chills.

"You sure you want this conversation?" He said, his eyes finally reaching mine.

"Yep." I said nodding my head. He couldn't tell, but my hands were sweating, and the wall I was leaning against was the only thing holding me up.

This time he nodded, biting his bottom lip. Getting up from his chair, I watched as he slowly made his way over to me. The closer he got the harder it was for me to breath.Swallowing loudly, I waited for him t approach me. I finally exhaled when he made it to me, chest to chest. I watched him as he watched me, his eyes telling everything and nothing at the same time.

"You are the sexiest woman I have ever seen." He used his right hand to grip my neck, the pressure just right. "The way you carry yourself is a work of art. Your confidence would make a weak man doubt himself. The way you talk, laugh, smile, love hard, and have your crazy ass friends back. And your mind, shit." He paused. And then he slowly exhaled as he brought his lips closer to my ear, and his left hand gripped my waist. There was no doubt in my mind he felt me tremble from his touch. "It makes my dick hard at just the thought of you." Stepping closer, I felt how hard he was. Glancing down slightly, I licked my lips when I saw his dick pushing against his sweatpants showing a very impressive dick print. His grip tightened on my throat a little causing me to look up at him.

"Don't look at something you can't touch yet, Queen." He said as he started to kiss my neck when he reached that space between my neck and shoulder and bit down, I couldn't stop the moan that escaped my lips. I couldn't help the shudder that went through my body as he continued down to my left breast.I could feel his warm breath through my thin t-shirt and lace bra. When he let go of my neck and waist to cup both my titties in his hands.I couldn't help but rest my head against the wall and close my eyes and enjoying the pleasure he was causing. Quickly he stopped only to pull my shirt over my head and throw it behind him. I heard him whisper damn as he looked down at me, my chest heaving, nipples hard as hell, and the seat of my panties were so wet I'm pretty sure they were see-through from all the moisture.

"You better tell me to stop now before I go any further."

He said in between kisses as he made his way down my chest. My lack of response told him precisely what I thought of him stopping. Each hot kiss making my skin prickle, stopping at the waist of my sweat, he looked up at me as he pulled them down along with my black boy shorts. Stepping out of them, I watched as he held my panties to his nose and inhaled my scent.

SIXTEEN
CHANCE

On my knees in front of Queen, I was eye level with her pussy.Her waxed clean but glistening because she was so wet pussy was the only thing on my mind. Without looking I put her panties in my pocket for safe keeping and for a souvenir. I started kissing her right thigh, slowly making my way towards her pussy only to skip over it and kiss on her left. Her hand made its way to my side; she ran her hand over my scalp as she moaned in pleasure, her other hand pulling and plucking her nipple. I kissed the top of her pussy one last time before pulling back. Her eyes popped open immediately when she felt the warmth of my touch no longer close to her. I sat back on my knees, looking up at her.

"Why did you stop?" She said as she tried to catch her breath. As a man it made me feel like I was walking on cloud nine that I could bring her the smallest amount of pleasure by just my touch and kiss alone.

"I don't want to do this right here; for one, I won't be able to make you cum like I want to. For two, you deserve better than to get fucked in the kitchen, at least for the first time. So, we are going to your room to finish this." I said as I got up off the floor.I expected her to become shy, withdraw from the thought of things getting out of hand because we hadn't discussed anything sexual. The few times I thought we were going to go there, we were interrupted, and we never discussed it. Tomy surprise, she took my hand and led me to her room. I watched her ass the entire short walk and as she slowly climbed into the bed. The only time she looked back at me, I wanted to drop to my knees again, but this time to thank the man upstairs. She made her way to the headboard and leaned back against it, dropping her legs wide open to give me the perfect view of her pussy. Making my way to her, I positioned myself in between her and kissed my way up her leg. I grabbed on to her thighs, wrapping my arms under them to get better leverage and to apply more pleasure to her clit. Rotating between kissing and biting softly up her leg, her moans grew louder with each touch of my lips as I made my way up. When I finally made it to her pussy, I could hear her breathing loudly above my head; I licked my lips and dove right in. I took one long lick from the clit to her outer labia; her soft whimpers turned to loud damn yelling moans as I licked, pulled, and sucked her pussy until her legs began to shake.

"Be still." I said, pulling back slightly and smacking her pussy to get her attention. Her mouth is hanging open slightly, but before she could say anything, I was back at it. Most men will tell you they gave head to women to get them ready for sex, but for me, it was an experience all to itself. I felt one of her hands on my head trying to direct me where she wanted me to be. Her other hand gripping the streets as she tried to control the pleasure, I was giving her. As if she had some type of control over the situation. I forewarned her earlier that I was in control of this. This was step one of learning her body, which stimulated her soul and caused her body to whimper with pleasure. I used my tongue to flick fast then slowly against her small pearl, flattening my tongue. I worked her more quickly as I added two fingers inside of her. I used my left hand to palm her stomach to keep her body from arching too far off the bed. Her nut hit her so fast and hard I wasn't prepared for her legs to clamp down against my head.

"You gotta stop Chance; I can't take to much more." She said as she tried to push my head away from her as her second nut started to build. Her body began to shake again, her back arched off the bed, and just as I started to pull back, she pulled me closer. I slurped and sucked on her until I heard her scream out my name and I felt my face become moist as she squirted in my face. Pulling back, I stood up and wiped my face with my shirt and smirked at her. Her face flushed, eye closed and chest heaving as she tried to get herself together and catch her breath.

"The condoms are in the top drawer." She said pointing over to her nightstand that sat next to her bed.

"Nah, baby that was it for the night. I'm going to shower; I'll be right back." I said as I pulled my shirt that was soaked with her juices over my head.

"What the hell are you talking about?" She said, popping up onto her elbows to look at me. Her face scrunched up from confusion.

"You heard what I said." I told her as I stripped down to my boxers. I watched as her eyes traveled along my body, only stopping at my dick. She licked her lips and continued up to my eyes.

"I heard you. I just don't believe you, and little Chance doesn't either because I can see I have his attention." She said finally sitting all the way up. The glow from the moon shining through her window added only to her sex appeal.

"Man, stop playing with me ain't shit little about my man here." I said, laughing as I gripped my dick. I walked around with seven inches on soft and ten on hard; if anything was small about me, it wasn't my dick. Waving her off, I headed towards the bathroom connected to her bedroom.

"You're serious, aren't you?" She yelled as I turned on the shower water.

"Hell yeah, I'm serious. Change your clothes and go to sleep. I'll be out in a minute." I yelled back to her as I stepped into the shower. I heard her talking to herself as drawers were yanked open and slammed shut. Laughing, I looked around her shower at her different body washes, picking up the one that by the description would smell the least girly I opened it. The smell of cocoa butter filled my nose just as the shower door was pulled open.

"Here's a towel." She said, standing there watching me as the water ran down my body. I made my dick, which was still hard jump just to give her a show.

"Thank you, now close the door." I said, taking the towel from her hand. She rolled her eyes yet didn't look away from me. So, to add to her torture, I stepped to stand under the water, allowing it to run down my body. Facing her, I lathered up my towel with soap and began washing my body, never taking my eyes off her the entire time. Washing my upper body first, she watched my hand closely when I ran the towel down my stomach, and to my dick, I heard her whimper as I started stroking myself. She watched the entire time as I jacked myself off. Never moving from her spot against the counter. In my mind, I pictured Queen's mouth was working my dick instead of my hand. With each pump, I came closer and closer to my nut. Pumping fast, I grunted as I ejaculated, shooting it down the drain.

"Shame, I would've swallowed all of that." Queen said as she watched me pull myself together. I looked over at her as she shrugged her shoulders and headed back towards the room. Laughing, I cleaned myself up and washed like I had common sense. Once I got out, put on lotion, wrapping myself in a towel I noticed my backpack sitting on top of the toilet lid. Pulling out an extra pair of underwear, shorts, and socks, I got dressed and headed into the room. Climbing into bed I pulled Queen close to me, her back against my front.

"Why are you wet?" I said to her and I draped my leg over her to get more comfortable.

"I took a shower in the guest bathroom after I grabbed your bag out your trunk. I remembered you said you always kept a bag in the trunk because your brothers always pop up wanting to play basketball. I you would need a change of clothes. I hope you don't mind." She said as she pushed her body closer to mine.

"Nope, thank you for doing that, you didn't have to." I said, kissing the back of her head. Her hair was tied up in a satin bonnet that I knew every black woman in my life seemed to own.

"Welcome." She said I could feel her breathing starting to even out as sleep began to take over. I was right behind her; I could feel my eye lips starting to get heavy.

"By the way, I was serious about what I said in the bathroom. Next time don't be so selfish." She mumbled halfway sleep.

"Take yo nasty ass to sleep, Queen." I said, laughing and

pulling her body closer to mine. Sleep both found us both shortly afterwards.

Pulling the cover higher up on our bodies, I rolled over to keep the sun out of my face. Queen snuggled closer to my body as if she had the same idea. I didn't even know what time it was nor did I care as long as I got to lay with here a little longer. Sometime during the night, we had moved, now I was laying on my back with her body draped across me.

"YOU KNOW mama is gonna be in here in a little bit, and the last thing she is going to want to see is you lying here with some man." A voice said from our feet, quickly Queen pulled the covers off her face and sat up which caused me to do the same thing. Protectively I pulled her behind me as much as I could.

"What the hell are you doing here?" She said to the woman who laid across the bench at the end of her bed. Her relaxed posture and bright smile were almost infectious.

"Well, I got into town last night and let myself in through the garage, and I noticed his car. I thought you finally bought a new one." She stopped talking and side-eyed me. Waiting for a response to her unspoken question, when we didn't reply, she kept talking. "So, I came to wake you up, but I noticed him in the bed with you. I thought it would be better if I waited until a decent time." She said, her striking features and dark skin I could tell she was Queen's sister, plus I'd seen I don't know how many pictures of her throughout her home.

"But anyway, your mama just called me and said she would be here within the next two hours, so I'm trying to get your hot to trot ass up before she gets here." Turning her attention to me she smiled at me and got up to head towards the door. "Hey, I'm Tommy, her oldest sister; it is beautiful to meet you, but I meant what I said, roll out before the royal highness brings her ass here. I don't know how much you have heard about her mother, but I am not in the mood to deal with her judgmental ass today. So, get a move on."

When she closed the door behind her, I turned back to Queen, who sat there with her face in her hands. Laying back, I pulled her down with me; she relaxed into my body as I played with her hair. Sometime during the night her bonnet had come off, allowing her locs to be free.

"We share the same parents, both of them. She only refers to her as my mother if she's pissed her off. Which means this is about to be a long day, especially since they're both here a few days early." She said, her eyes focused on the tree right outside her window.

"It'll be fine, watch what I tell you." I said as I played with her locs.

"You don't know my mama, that woman knows what button to push and when. It's easier not to encourage her bullshit and stay in your own little world."

SEVENTEEN
QUEEN

Chance and I made our way to the master bathroom; he didn't rush around like he was afraid he was going to get caught by my parents, nor was he ashamed that Tommy had seen him. He carried on with what I assumed was his morning routine as if he was at home. I stood at the counter, the same side like last night, while I brushed my teeth and watched him behind me go through his gym bag that he'd left sitting neatly against the wall out the way. He stood next to me as he washed his face, brushed his teeth, and flossed. Every so often he'd peer over at me and smile or wink at me. When he finally stepped in the shower, I headed towards the living room where I had no doubt Tommy would be.

"You could have text and told me you were here instead of waking us up, you know." I said to her as I threw a throw pillow at her head that was sitting on the floor. Knowing Tommy, she had intentionally thrown the pillows on the story to move my focus from her to her mild attempt to junky up my living room.

"What fun would that be?" She said rolling to her side

and falling off the couch as she tried to getaway. I stepped over the back of the couch and stood above her hitting her with a pillow.

"You live to torture me, Thomasina McDaniel," I said, hitting her repeatedly as she laughed and tried to ball herself into the fetal position.

"I thought I was doing you a favor and allowing you to get your back blown out!" She said as she continued to laugh at me.

"Yeah, right," I said, hitting her one last time as I stepped down off the couch. Her loud laughing ass struggled to get up off the floor as I walked away from her and headed into the kitchen.

"He's the one you've been telling me about, isn't he?" She said as she flopped down on the couch, I was just standing on.

"Yes." I said cutting my eyes from her to the hallway that lead to my bedroom.

"He's cute." She said, shrugging her shoulders.

"He very much so is." I said, nodding as I opened the fridge and grabbed a bottle of orange juice with one hand a bowl of fruit with the other. I used my left foot to close the door, my full attention on my fruit salad, I was prepared to eat.

"Then introduce him to the family." She said offhandedly as she picked up her mess.

"That definitely isn't going to happen. He meet them?" I said as I pulled open the drawer, I kept my silverware in. The entire time I shook my head no. "Not even going to lie, I had no plans to have him meet you. That man and our family? No ma'am that is not about to happen. Two different types of people in two different worlds. You think I'm about to listen to Emmerson run her mouth for God knows how long after she sees him? Yeah, fucking right, I love my peace, and she would try to destroy that after seeing him." When she didn't respond right off, I turned to see Chance standing there. The look of confusion and anger evident on his face, there was no doubt in my mind he heard what I was saying to Tommy.

"I'm about to head out." He said after a few seconds of silence, his facial expression went from happy to sad to disappointment with a blink of an eyee.Adjusting his bag, he turned, grabbed his keys off the end table, and headed towards the door. He gave Tommy acknowledgment as a head nod on the way out.

"Why didn't you tell me he was here." I said to her as I wiped my hands on a table and rushed around the center island. She looked at me dumb founded, opened and closed her mouth then shrugged her shoulders. She was as lost as I was. When I made it to the garage, he was just putting his bags in the back seat. He looked up at me as I hit the switch to close the door, he damn near broke the window of his back door from slamming it so hard.

"I need to get to the shop; can you open the garage, please?" He said, barely looking up at me as he opened his front door.

"Can we talk for a second?" I asked making my way towards him. I took cautious steps; it wasn't as if I was afraid, he would hit me because I knew him well enough to know he wouldn't. I just didn't want him to feel like I was overstepping my boundaries and invading his personal space.

"Nah I'm good, I got shit to do." He said dismissively as he got into the car. He wouldn't even look at me.

"Can I call you later?" I said to him as my hand hovered over the button. I watched as he put his shades on, adjusted his baseball cap, and gripped the hell out of the steering wheel after he hit the push start for his car. I watched as he backed out the driveway, not once glancing back to look at me. When he was out of sight I headed back into the house, flopping down on the couch, I leaned my head back against the back of the sofa and let out a heavy sigh.

"Care to explain to me why you said what you did?" Tommy said as she sat down next to me.

"Mama will get one look at him with his tattoo's, vampire fanged dipped grill which by the way he doesn't often wear because I've only seen pictures of him when he has them on, but goodness is it sexy. The hood style clothing let alone hear his vernacular. And it won't matter how smart he is, how talented he is, how sweet he is. She won't care that he texts me every day to make sure I'm awake and on time for work like I'm not one of the ones who's always on time, and he's late. He calls me at night when we aren't hanging out just to ask about my day. It won't matter to her that he's incredible and funny or that he can make anyone in the room feel like the sun revolves around them. All she will do is try to find fault in everything that he is." I said without looking at her; I kept my eye closed the entire time I spoke. If I hadn't I would have definitely cried. I knew how fucked up it sounded to him without the explanation, but he hadn't given me the chance to.

"And he doesn't deserve that." She said, gently hitting my shoulder with her shoulder to cheer me up. She of all people knew what it was like to deal with our mother and her constant nagging and outright dislike of a lifestyle or person's perception of how they should be seen or act.

"Nope, but he's not in the right frame of mind to hear that. I'll give him a minute to calm down, and then I'll tell him what I meant." I said as I got up off the couch, I heard her simple okay as a response as I made my way towards my bedroom. I laid down in the bed, his smell still fresh on my pillow and covers. Putting the pillow over my head, I closed my eyes, his look of disappointment and anger still fresh on my mind.

Chance

"All three of you fools are sitting around here looking like some damn lost puppies because of some women." My pops said as he cut into his steak.My family had been in town all of three days, and I was ready for them to go back home. For the past few days, I'd been able to bury myself in work and ignore the world. When my mom said, it was time to have family dinner, my pops dragged all our asses out the door and into the car and dared any of us to say anything. It would give him an excuse to cuss us out or try and beat our asses.

"Charles, leave them alone." My mom said as she looked around the restaurant. This was our first time at the steak house, and if I were paying attention to my meal more, I could say I enjoyed it, but my mind was elsewhere.

"Nah, Charlene, look at them, all looking stupid as hell." He said pointing his knife at each of us. "You listened to your bitter ass brother years ago and let your woman getaway. Now you're sitting here moping around because she doesn't want you, which I don't blame her for. Your dumb ass been letting that girl run off whenever she felt like it, and she's gone once again and for how long we don't even fucking know. And what did she do? Ran her big head ass off without a word like always and expect you to stay behind, twiddling your fingers waiting on her to turn that damn location on and for you to jump up like a damn dog and go to her." He said, pointing at Choice then Channing, what he said was right, and we all knew it. "And you? I'm not even sure why you're sitting here looking dumb as a box of rocks, but whatever it is, you probably deserve it because you're a whore, so whatever woman broke your little heart, I want to buy her a damn drink." He said pointing at me.

"Well damn pop tell them how you really feel why don't you." My sister Charity said as she tried to cover her laughter up. She failed miserably, so she leaned into our mothers' shoulder and laughed. Mama didn't do anything but pat her head and continue eating; she was used to our father and his honest parenting tactics.

"Oh, you shut up over there, I haven't even started in on you yet. Keep on sounding like a damn duck with all that quacking over there." He said, waving her off; her laughter immediately stopped, which caused our mom to start up laughing.

"Look what your father is trying to say is you three are not the brightest bunch when it comes to the opposite sex and in your case Charity the same sex too. As smart as yall are, I have to agree with your father and say you're dumb as a box of rocks." She said, wiping her mouth with her napkin. All of us sat staring at her as if she'd grown another head. Usually, my father was the blunt one, but today it seemed like she was putting that hat on to wear.

"Damn, mama." Choice said leaning back into his chair and crossing his arms.

"I mean, we are used to him just telling us about ourselves, but you jumping in now?" Channing said as he looked back and forth between them.

"I'm just an innocent bystander in this little game yall call life. You could have left me out of it." Charity said, which caused all of us to just look at her.

"You a damn lie and a half," We all said at the same time, which caused her to fall over with laughter. It was no family secret that Charity told our parents everything she knew and wasn't ashamed of it. No matter if we swore her to secrecy or not, she sang like a damn bird every time our parents looked at her like she was crazy.

"So, tell me what's going on, Choice, we all know Anlee isn't giving you the time of day, which, like your father said, is understandable. Channing, we've told you I don't know how many times to either tell Jess how you feel about the situation or shut up and deal with it. Now you Chance, I'm pretty sure you're having a hard time with that girl you were telling me about a few months ago. And Charity, you just shut your confused ass up. I'm not even about to go in on your ass."

"What girl?" Pops asked he ignored the comments about everyone else. We'd been dealing with it for years, so their news wasn't news anymore.

"Nobody pops, she's not what I thought she was." I said, shaking my head. I wasn't trying to eavesdrop on Queen and Tommy's conversation the other day. I was heading into the living room to grab my work bag and head to the shop to prepare for my day. When I heard her telling her sister, she would never introduce me to her family was a swift kick to the nuts. We hadn't discussed meeting family, but she had met my brothers, and officially, I'd met Tommy that morning. But to hear her say she didn't want me to meet the rest of them? It did something to me.

"Queen is a girl he's been chasing behind since he met her a few months back. She hurt his feelings because he was ear hustling and heard her tell her sister he wasn't the type of nigga she would introduce to her people, so now he all in his damn feelings." Charity quickly said. I threw a piece of lettuce off my plate at her. I let out a small chuckle when she caught it and ate it, smiling the entire time brightly.

"If she doesn't see the great man you are, then she doesn't deserve you. Plus, her name sounds uppity anyway, who names her daughter Queen?" Pops said, pushing his empty plate towards the middle of the table.

"Daddy, didn't you just call him a whore not too long ago?" Charity said slightly confused.

"Shut the hell up, Charity, you always instigating shit." Choice said waving her off.

"Well he did! After he basically called you a dumb ass and Channing a punk." She said, shrugging.

"I told you Charlene; you should've swallowed them." Pop said to moms who simply nodded at him and continued staring off into the restaurant. Something behind me kept her focus the majority of the time we had been sitting down. It took everything in me not to laugh, but I couldn't stop it once I heard Channing start to laugh beside me the entire table irrupted in laughter. It was our parents running joke that whenever we got on their nerves, they would make that comment. Usually, our moms would try to act offended and tell pops it was inappropriate to say in front of us, but today she even laughed.

EIGHTEEN
QUEEN

"No, I absolutely have no desire to deal with anyone you are trying to set me up with," I said to my mom as I made my way through the restaurant to our seats. My family being in town usually wasn't this hard to bear, but my mother was on overdrive as she tried to plead her case. The steakhouse we were at was new in town but one of my favorites.

"I'm not seeing the problem with you just meeting him." She said as she waited for my dad to pull her seat out for her to sit. I glanced over at my siblings, who all tried to be invisible and stay off her radar. Emanuel pulled both mine and Tommy's chairs out and sat in between us, while Tempest's husband pulled hers out for her.

"I do, I'm not trying to be set up, I am enjoying my life. I don't understand why it is so hard for you to understand." I used the shield that was sat in front of me as a shield from her stare. The constant nagging was only going to get so far with me before I blew up. I felt my knee start to bounce as I tried to control myself.

"Queen, just meet him." She said, waving off my objection as if it was a gnat bugging her.

"And why not?" Tempest said as she sat her menu down on the table. I noticed the way she brushed her husbands' hand away from her. Glancing over at Tommy, she nodded her head towards them and raised her eyebrow in an unspoken question to me. It seemed like there were already problems in paradise.

"Because I don't want to, I am enjoying my life and don't see the point of adding some guy who I'm not interested in into my life just because you want me to." I said as I looked over the menu, I didn't have any idea on what I was going to eat because I really didn't have an appetite. I would rather be in bed , ignoring the world because I wanted to be with Chance, but he hadn't returned my calls or text.

"You arewasting your prime years away for absolutely no reason besides the fact that you're trying to be stubborn because I'm suggesting it."

"Or she could just not be interested in some boring guy you think is good for the look for how you want to be perceived." Emanuel said as he sat his menu down. If looks could kill he'd be dead from the look that was shot at him from our mom.His response was a simple shrug as he drank some of his water that had been given to us when we first sat down.

"You have no room to talk; you own a sex club for whores and sadists." Tempest said with the same disdain in her voice as our mom had.

"It's definitely not for whores and sadist," Tommy said, laughing.

"How would you know?" Slamming down her menu, my mom looked between them as if the thought of Tommy dealing with Emanuel's business was beyond comprehension. "Have you been there before? Are you a member?"

I half-listened as they began to argue between them

Tommy and Emanuel on one side and mom and Tempest on the other. The entire time my dad typed away at his phone, used to the constant arguing, and ignoring it like he always did. Tuning them out, I took in the look of the restaurant, the hickory floors with brick walls didn't clash with the metal and cedar tables and booths. Each table had hanging pendant vintage-looking lights that gave each table its intimate feel without trying to be overly sexy.

"He's in the corner to your left." I heard Tommy whisper to me; I didn't need to ask her who or what she was talking about. Turning my head slightly to the left, I watched as Chance and his family sat and talked amongst themselves. They looked to be enjoying themselves, I saw pictures of his parents and sister, even if I hadn't, they all looked so much alike it was no way that they could try to deny they were related. From my viewpoint, I could see him, but he couldn't see me; his mother noticed me looking and gave a slight head nod in acknowledgment. After returning the nod, I pulled my attention back to my family and tried to endure the remainder of the evening.

THE NEXT MORNING, I sat at another restaurant with my mom and sisters, but this time, I was ready to knock everything over and storm out. My dad and Emanuel were checking out Emanuel's newest investment and then swinging by his house to see it was coming a long before meeting us here. I sat next to Tommy, trying to get my anger under control as I listened to my mom introduce to us two different men; she had invited to join us.

"These are the two men I mentioned last night at dinner Eugene Carver and Mathew Eddleston, they own a real estate company, and these are my daughters Thomasina and Queen." She said, pointing us out; her bright smile showed no remorse. I felt Tommy grab my leg under the table to stop it from bouncing up and down. Tempest sat there smiling brighter than our mom, which let me know she was in on this setup.

"It's nice to meet you, and I'm sure you are very nice men, but I am not interested. I'm not sure what she told you or what she promised you, but no, just no." Standing, I wiped my hands on my napkin and set it down. Grabbing my purse, keys, and phone, I didn't even wait for anyone to respond as I headed for the door. I could hear her and my sisters calling my name as I left but I didn't even stop. It only hit me once I was in the parking lot that I didn't drive, but it didn't matter I wasn't far from Emanuel's business so I headed that way, hoping him and my father hadn't left yet. I cut through the park and was on main street before I realized it, the entire time I replayed the last few conversations with my mom over in my head. She was overstepping her boundaries and was desperate for something that I wasn't worried about.

When I made it to The Cigar Club, I let out a sigh of relief when I saw my brothers' car was still parked in front of the building. But that sigh quickly turned into a groan of frustration when my parent's rental and another car pulled up and parked right next to it. Throwing my hands in the arm in frustration, I made my way over to the bench and sat down. I could hear my mom's heels clicking against the concrete as she made her way over towards me.

"Queen, what is your problem? That was not only rude but absolutely uncalled for. Eugene and Mathew are only here because I asked them to come." She said, standing directly in front of me; when she would chastise me the same way. She always stood over me; she wasn't a tall woman she stood maybe five-three on a good day, my siblings got our height from our dad. We towered over her by the time we were twelve, so she began standing over us when we sat down to make it seem like she wasn't as short as she was.

"I didn't ask you to bring them here, mama." I said dropping my head into my hands, the anger and disrespect I felt at this moment was almost too much to bear. She wasn't going to stop, no matter how much I asked nice or ignored the problem. She had her mind set up on marrying me off and soon.

"What?" She said as if she hadn't heard me when I knew she did. From the shadow on the ground, I could see her put her hands on her hips and widen her stance a little to prepare for a battle she knew she wouldn't lose.

"Emmerson leave her be; come on now." My dad said as he walked towards her. We had been speaking a lot more lately, and I let him know how overbearing she was becoming. He said he would step in when he saw it was becoming too much for any of us to handle.

"I will not! She needs to get herself together and come and apologize. I didn't fly them out here to be treated this way." She said to him, to onlookers, I knew we were starting to make a scene, but I didn't care.

"You flew who out here?" Emanuel said as he tried to gather what the hell was going on. Looking up I saw the confusion on his face and shook my head. Of course, she would bring them here; she hadn't mentioned them last night at dinner. This was way more than just some hook up. This was a planned out and precisely executed.

"It's none of your business; this concerns your sisters. Stay out of it!" She said through clenched teeth to Emanuel, who only looked at her as if she had lost her damn mind, which in my opinion she had.

"Emmerson you need to chill out. What is wrong with you?" Dad said grabbing hold of her arm to make her face him. In all the years I've been alive I've never seen him this angry.

"Nothing is wrong with me, Thomas! It's your ungrateful daughter who is sitting there being rude and storming off at restaurants instead of meeting the man I have been telling her about for weeks!" She yelled at him as she pointed at me. Her face red with anger, her breathing uneven as she looked from me to him.

"I'm ungrateful? How?! I didn't ask for any of this! I have told you I don't know how many times I'm not interested in anyone you have mentioned. I don't know how many times I have to say this!" Standing, I walked towards my siblings to get away from her; what part of this entire thing she didn't find fucked up was beyond me. Shaking her head Tommy grabbed my hand to make sure I stayed next to her, her silent support, and protest of our mama's behavior.

"You flew two men out here to meet Tommy and me without our permission. More than likely told them some bullshit and had them excited to meet us and now look at them over there, looking dumber than a box of rocks because they don't know what's going on!"

"She did what?!" Emanuel said, turning to face me then Mathew and Eugene, who still stood next to the car looking lost as hell. The fact they didn't object to anything that was said spoke volumes in itself. At this point, I didn't even know who which man was, they both looked like they would rather be somewhere else than in the middle of our fucked-up family argument. Shaking his head Emanuel started back to his car; he pulled his passenger door open with so much force he shook his car. He sat down in the seat, grabbing his black backpack he always kept with him. I looked over at Tommy, who was just as lost as I was.

"What did she tell yall?" Tommy asked her attention off Emanuel, who looked as if he was ready to blow at any given moment. He had the worst temper out of all of us, years of anger management had done nothing for him. He still would go off on anyone at any time; people always thought otherwise because of his usual calm demeanor.

"That you two were interested, you would play hard to get in the beginning, but it wouldn't matter in the end. We could pick whomever we wanted." One said, he looked like he was ready to run for the hills at any given moment. He didn't seem like he was a bad guy, just dumb to be in this situation.

"We aren't interested, like at all." Tommy said as she shook her head and leaned against the glass of The Cigar Club's window front.

"She said you were possibly going through a phase of liking women and would be harder to deal with. But on the flight here we looked you both up, I told Eugene that I wanted to deal with you Queen, you seemed more like my speed. Docile and calm, Eugene was okay with that." The other said, now he looked like he was an asshole. The way he stood there as if we were beneath him, his face turned up like he smelled something sour.

"I cannot deal with this shit." Shaking my head, I wiped my hands down my face. This was becoming too much.

"I am not gay! And if I was who the fuck cares! You are ridiculous." Tommy said, turning her attention to our mom, who had the nerve to look as if she had done nothing wrong. She stood next to dad, arms crossed over her chest, back straight, head held high. The things she did were borderline crazy, and she needed to be evaluated.

"You will deal with whatever I say you will. This entire outburst you are having is uncalled for. Was your mother wrong for not telling you we were coming yes, but this temper tantrum you are throwing is unnecessary." Mathew said, I was right. He was a dick. "No future wife of mine will act this way especially in public, now get over here." He snapped his fingers at me and pointed to the spot next to him. The audacity and arrogance made everyone standing around, stop, and stare.

I quickly made my way towards Emanuel who had pulled his gun out of his bag and cocking it. He pointed it directly at Mathew. My big brother did not play with the disrespect, mainly when it was directed at one of us. The way he decided to handle things that got him into a lot of trouble when we were younger.

"Please don't, he's not worth it. Think about Kory; you can't do something like this. You have to think about her now. I'm a big girl I can handle this." I did the dumbest thing I could think of, I stepped in front of him the gun barrel aimed straight at my heart. It didn't matter though; I had to get his attention and keep it. I wasn't protecting anyone but Emanuel at this point. I knew he would never hurt me, but I didn't doubt for one minute he'd pull the trigger and shoot Mathew if he said the wrong thing. I had to appeal to reason when it came to Emanuel, and the mention of Kory was the only thing that would grab and keep his attention.

"Come on, Emanuel, think son." Our dad's voice of reason came from beside us; I never heard or saw him move from next to my mom, but he had.

"Yeah, Emanuel let it go; it's not worth it," Tommy said.

NINETEEN
CHANCE

The constant buzz of my phone pulled me out of the small amount of sleep I was getting on the couch in my office at the shop. After leaving the restaurant, I wasn't in the mood to deal with the constant noise and chatter of my family, so I decided to hang out at the shop for a little. My parents were set for the night and I had no reason to rush home to them. So I ended up crashing on the couch for the night. Finally, grabbing my phone, I noticed the twenty missed calls and twelve unread text messages majority from a number I didn't know and a few from my parents. Throwing the phone back on the couch, I stood stretching my tall frame and headed to the bathroom to pee, brush my teeth, and take a quick shower.

My day went by smoothly; my scheduled appointments and a few walk-ins kept me busy. I had a few appointments tomorrow that I had to do, but I wasn't overbooked. Turning on the music I blasted out the outside noise from the lobby and other art music.

"I wanted to talk to you about what we were discussing

last night." My mom said as she closed the door behind her, I figured she would eventually make her way to the shop to talk. She never let us stew in our problems alone too much, she wasn't overbearing and knew her boundaries, but she was a believer in talking your questions out.

"There's nothing to really discuss," I said as I got up to hug her. Her warm vanilla scent she always wore wrapped me in a tighter embrace than her actual arms.

"That's not entirely true and you know it." She said, patting my back; when she let me go, she watched me closely as I made it back around to my desk. I didn't sit down until she did. When I didn't say anything right off, she mimicked my posture by sitting back in her chair and crossing her arms over her chest.

"Mama, I don't know what you want me to say." Rubbing my hands down my face as I let out a frustrated breath.

"The truth love, say your truth." She said the understanding and compassion in her voice made me drop my head on the desk. How was I to explain that my feelings were hurt by a woman I wasn't even in a relationship with.

"Ma, come on." My voice was muffled from my face being smashed against my desk. I could hear her soft laughter, which made me raise my head off the desk to see her face.

"Son, you obviously have something on your chest that you need to get off. Now I can be your listening ear, or your father could be, and we both know exactly how that is going to play out."

"He will call me dumb and tell me it's all my fault because I've been a whore in the past, and this is just karma coming back to bite me in the ass." Laughing I said as I leaned all the way back in my seat. Mama slight head nod told me she completely agreed with my comment. Letting out a deep sigh I nodded my head, if I was going to get it off my chest I might as well tell the person who would actually listen and give me her sound opinion on the subject.

"Hey man, come on your girl out here with a gun pointed at her!" Channing said, rushing into my office, both mama and I turned to look at him like he was crazy. Bent over with his hands on his knee's he looked up at us as if we knew what he was talking about.

"Nigga Queen is outside with a fucking gun pointed at her! I don't care what she said to you the other day get your ass up!" Standing he rushed back out the room just as quickly as he came. Without thinking I grabbed my gun out my top drawer and took off right behind him. I could hear Mama calling for Choice and pops telling them back up was needed, even though she had never met Queen she knew how I felt about her.

When I got outside, my heart dropped right out of my chest, where she was standing in front of some nigga who had a gun pointed directly at her chest. Her sister Tommy stood next to her; on the other side of her, some older nigga stood. They were all talking to the nigga with the gun; he never took his eyes off Queen. It was like everything happen in slow motion as I made my way to her.

"Queen!" I yelled her name; she never turned to face me, just put her hand up and nodded her head, still talking to the nigga with the gun. As he lowered the gun, some dude behind her pushed past her and ran away; I watched as she lost her balance from the force of him pushing pass her and stumbled off the curb. No matter how fast I was running and short the distance was between us I couldn't stop her from falling, since her attention wasn't on the man behind her, she never got a chance to prepare herself. I watched in horror as she fell into the street, the car moving pass her never had a chance to swerve. Her body was clipped by the passenger side of the car, she jerked sideways from the force of the car and landed on her side right at the curb, her head hitting the ground.

TWENTY
EMANUEL

I know better than to let someone else get the better of me; it took me years of therapy to figure out my triggers. My short temper was the main reason I stayed to myself most of the time, I had a problem with disrespect, especially if it involved women. So, as I listen to my mama and sister argue, I kept having to remind myself to stay out of it and sta y calm. But when he told Queen to come to him. Something inside of me snapped. I don't even remember pulling my gun. I do remember the look in my sisters' eyes as she pleaded with me to put it away. I remember her mentioning Kory. I even remember someone calling her name, but she never took her eyes off me, she spoke soft and calmly as she told me her plans after this was over. The smile she had on her face was full of love as she told me that the guy who was calling her name was the one she had been seeing for the past few months, and she thought she was falling in love with him. I wanted to point out that from the look on hisface and the concern in his voice that they were already past the like phase. I had just lowered when that punk-ass Eugene pushed past us and ran away. When he did, I tried to reach out and grab her, to catch her before she fell, but I didn't get to her in time. The car came out of nowhere, and I watched as she was hit. Her body bounced off the car and hit the street.

"Queen! Come on, baby, get up!" The man that had yelled her name said as he rolled her over gently. Blood was coming out her ear, and out the gash, she had on her forehead. "Yo, someone call 911! Hurry up!" His attention on Queen as he pulled his shirt off and pressed it to her wound.In the distance, I could hear the ambulance in the. The people he was with pushed pass me to help him; they never tried to move her once they had her on her back.

"Chance she's going to be okay, just keep talking to her." An older woman held her neck in place so her head wouldn't move, she spoke to the man I figured was her son in a calm voice. Every so often she would look up at us, I guess trying to figure out why we hadn't moved.

I could hear him whispering to her, the entire time he stayed down on his knees, his mouth inches from her ear. Whatever he was saying seemed like the most important thing in the world to him. When the ambulance arrived, they yelled stuff out to each other and to us, trying to figure out what happens. The driver of the car stood next to it crying her eyes off, she just kept saying she never saw Queen there. Tommy pops, and the nigga who ran to her rescue all got in with Queen to ride to the hospital. Tempest, Mathew, and our mom stood to the side the entire time. Watching as if the situation wasn't serious.

"If she doesn't make it, I'm going to make sure you go away for life." My mom said to me as she walked past me. Tempest and Mathew got into the car; they pulled off and drove the opposite direction of the ambulance.

"We are heading to the hospital if you would like to ride

with us." The older woman said she touched my arm gently to get my attention.

"This is all my fault." I said to her as I looked down at her hand.

"No, baby, it's not. Who is she to you?"

"My kid sister. I wasn't going to shoot her, that nigga that just walked away with our mom. Yeah, I would haveput a bullet in him for the disrespect. She stood in the way so I wouldn't do it. She knows I would never hurt her; she was saving that nigga."

"And she knew that that's why she stood in front of you. Now come on, you're in no shape mentally to be driving you can ride with us." Grabbing my hand, she pulled me with her towards a waiting SUV. When we got in, no one said a word, the older man who I assumed was her husband pulled off onto the street after checking me out in the review mirror for a few seconds.

"Okay, okay, yeah we on our way now. Yeah nigga damn! Get off my fucking phone Chance we be there in a minute." Hanging up the phone, the man next to me dropped his head down against the back of the seat. He or the man in the back didn't even look over at me or acknowledge me the entire car ride. The ride to the hospital took no time; we found a spot close to the door and rushed inside. It didn't take me long to find them, I heard Tommy's screaming voice as soon I stepped inside the emergency room.

"Queen! No, save my sister!" Pops held her tightly as he pulled her out of the room, and the nurse closed the curtain behind them. Each tear that rolled down her face crushed my heart more and more. The closer I got to them, the more I heard coming from behind the curtain, the urgency of the doctors, and nurses working and yelling orders. The curtain was pulled back just as quick as it was closed, the doctors and nurses rushing pass us as the pushed Queen towards the elevator.

"We have to take her up to emergency surgery she had some internal bleeding from being hit by the car, and her brain is swelling, so we need to relieve the pressure." A doctor said to pops, he walked and talked so I knew the situation was serious. He simply nodded and held on to Tommy, who still was crying uncontrollably. I watched as the elevator doors opened and they all got on, as the doors closed, we heard one the doctors yell "She's coding!"

SUBSCRIBE

Text Grand to 31996 to stay up to date with new releases, sneak peeks, contest, reading groups and more....

SOME JOIN OUR TEAM!!!

To submit your manuscript to Grand Penz Publications, please send the first three chapters and synopsis to grandpenzpublications@gmail.com

www.ingramcontent.com/pod-product-compliance
Ingram Content Group UK Ltd.
Pitfield, Milton Keynes, MK11 3LW, UK
UKHW021912190726
13853UKWH00002B/630